MW01254895

HELL DIFFICULTY TUTORIAL

VOLUME I

WRITTEN BY
CERIM

ART BY
OMOY

AETHON
BOOKS

vault

HELL DIFFICULTY TUTORIAL
VOLUME 1

WRITTEN BY
CERIM

ART BY
OMOY

AETHON
BOOKS

vault

EDITORIAL
ADRIAN WASSEL — CCO & EDITOR-IN-CHIEF
DER-SHING HELMER — MANAGING EDITOR

DESIGN & PRODUCTION
TIM DANIEL — EVP, DESIGN & PRODUCTION
ADAM CAHOON — SENIOR DESIGNER & PRODUCTION ASSOCIATE
NATHAN GOODEN — CO-FOUNDER & SENIOR ARTIST

SALES & MARKETING
DAVID DISSANAYAKE — VP, SALES & MARKETING
SYNDEE BARWICK — DIRECTOR, BOOK MARKET SALES
BRITTA BUESCHER — DIRECTOR, SOCIAL MEDIA

OPERATIONS & STRATEGY
DAMIAN WASSEL — CEO & PUBLISHER
CHRIS KANALEY — CSO
F.J. DESANTO — HEAD OF FILM & TV

HELL DIFFICULTY TUTORIAL, VOLUME 1, MAY, 2025 COPYRIGHT © 2025, CERIM. ALL RIGHTS RESERVED. "HELL DIFFICULTY TUTORIAL",
HELL DIFFICULTY TUTORIAL LOGO, AND THE LIKENESSES OF ALL CHARACTERS HEREIN ARE TRADEMARKS OF CERIM, UNLESS OTHERWISE
NOTED. "VAULT" AND THE VAULT LOGO ARE TRADEMARKS OF VAULT STORYWORKS LLC. "AETHON BOOKS" AND THE AETHON BOOKS LOGO
ARE TRADEMARKS OF AETHON BOOKS, LLC. NO PART OF THIS WORK MAY BE REPRODUCED, TRANSMITTED, STORED OR USED IN ANY
FORM OR BY ANY MEANS GRAPHIC, ELECTRONIC, OR MECHANICAL, INCLUDING BUT NOT LIMITED TO PHOTOCOPYING, RECORDING,
SCANNING, DIGITIZING, TAPING, WEB DISTRIBUTION, INFORMATION NETWORKS, OR INFORMATION STORAGE AND RETRIEVAL SYSTEMS,
EXCEPT AS PERMITTED UNDER SECTION 107 OR 108 OF THE 1976 UNITED STATES COPYRIGHT ACT, WITHOUT THE PRIOR WRITTEN PER-
MISSION OF THE PUBLISHER. ALL NAMES, CHARACTERS, EVENTS, AND LOCALES IN THIS PUBLICATION ARE ENTIRELY FICTIONAL. ANY RE-
SEMBLANCE TO ACTUAL PERSONS (LIVING OR DEAD), EVENTS, INSTITUTIONS, OR PLACES, WITHOUT SATIRIC INTENT, IS COINCIDENTAL.
PRINTED IN USA. FOR INFORMATION ABOUT FOREIGN OR MULTIMEDIA RIGHTS, CONTACT: RIGHTS@VAULTCOMICS.COM

TABLE OF CONTENTS

CHAPTER 1
BORING COMMUTE

I let out a small yawn, my cheek pressed against the cool bus window. For a brief moment, a streetlight blinds me, forcing me to close my eyes. When the light fades, another yawn escapes from me.

Shifting my gym bag, I wriggle into a more comfortable position and sneak a peek toward the front of the half-full bus.

A standing boy mutters something, and his friends erupt in laughter. One of them, in particular, lets out a laugh that's... Well, it's unique. He continues to cackle without a care in the world.

Honestly, it's beginning to freak me out a bit. Seriously, what's the deal with that laugh?

As I tear my gaze away from them, I catch the eye of a girl around my age of twenty-one, sitting a few seats behind the noisy bunch. Annoyance is etched on her face.

Our eyes lock for a moment, and then we both nod. Just like that, an eternal bond is forged between us, united

in our annoyance by the gaggle of kids but too lazy to do anything about it.

For a bit, I observe an older lady holding a somewhat cheeky-looking corgi. Then I nod at the blond girl, my old friend Tess, and she waves at me before turning her attention back to the petite, black-haired girl she is talking to.

An older, strict-looking man catches my gaze, but we both quickly turn away.

When I get bored, I return my attention to the window, and for a moment, I look at my reflection in it. Messy hair, a face that is almost perpetually expressionless, and two differently colored eyes—one gray and the other brown.

Such a handsome young lad!

Then I close my eyes, and through my closed eyelids, I see the rhythmic flashes of streetlights as we pass by them. The hum of the bus and the muted conversations blend into a soothing white noise, lulling me toward sleep.

And then, suddenly, chaos erupts.

Blinding light.

A sensation of falling.

Terrified screams.

The flash of light is far more intense than any streetlight. The sensation is akin to the bus being hoisted into the air and dropped down.

Screams fill the air again, some quivering with fear, others laced with shock.

The cacophony of shattering glass and groaning metal assaults my ears. I open my eyes, only to squint as the overpowering light blinds me. My pupils dilate as they adjust to the brightness.

Daylight? What the heck?

I gape out the window at the blue sky and the sun peeking out from behind the clouds. If anyone asked, I'd swear it was morning or maybe early afternoon at the latest. But how could that be? It was late afternoon just moments ago.

"Let's calm down." The bus driver attempts to reassure the frantic passengers, but his efforts are in vain as the shouting continues.

Unlike the others, who have sprung to their feet, I remain in my seat, staring out the window. My gaze travels across the sky. A cold sweat trickles down my back as it dawns on me.

Uh, what? The hell? Is this some kind of hallucination? A dream? Something like this shouldn't be possible, right? I close my eyes and then reopen them. Nothing changes.

Well, this just got a whole lot more interesting.

Since when are there two suns in the sky? Did I hit my head? Is it a prank? How would you even pull off something like that?

The first sun is hiding behind the clouds, and the second...the second maybe-sun, smaller and more orange in color, beams in the sky to the left of the first one.

And where are all the buildings? Where is the road? The surrounding area is a clearing, encircled by tall trees and a lot of greenery. There are no hills or mountains, and the forest appears to stretch on endlessly.

Okay, let's calm down.

Slow and deep breaths.

In and out.

Good.

I hurriedly fish my phone out of my pocket, and of course, there's no signal. Not even a smidgen. Now what?

I glance at the other travelers and see that the first ones are already stepping outside. A few of them check their phones, but judging from their faces, they're also out of luck.

After grabbing my bag, I, too, exit the bus and step onto the grass... Yup, grass.

"What the hell?" I hear, and when I glance to my left, I see the annoyed girl from before, gawking at the second maybe-sun with her mouth agape.

Welcome to the club. No refunds.

Please send help.

"Sophie." A cute little girl holds the annoyed girl's hand.

"I'm sorry."

My gaze lands on the bus driver as I survey the area. He's still trying to calm down others. Must be some weird sense of responsibility or something. About ten people huddle around him. Then some kids, likely from the same school, stand near the bus. A few men, already forming a group, stand off to the side. A girl and her mini version are to my left, and two other women are nearby.

The small corgi barks as its head peeks out from the woman's arms.

Cute doggo.

"I have no idea what happened!" I hear the bus driver exclaim. "I don't know where we are."

Poor guy.

"Hey...hey!" I hear behind me as I move away from the bus, checking the signal on my phone.

It's the annoyed girl, and she stops when I turn toward her. I don't say anything, just wait for her to continue. She looks lost for words and simply asks, "Where are you

going?" while nervously glancing at the bus as if it's her lifeboat in the middle of the ocean.

"Just checking the signal," I say and show her the display on my phone.

After wandering for a while, but always keeping the bus in sight, I give up and turn off my phone. Better to conserve my battery. Thankfully, my battery is around 80 percent.

I glance at the second maybe-sun... Yeah.

Houston, we have a problem.

A little orange problem.

Well, if it's a sun, it isn't exactly little. It's probably larger than the planet, moon, or whatever we're on, but... I sigh and force myself to calm down.

If I pretend it's not there, it might vanish on its own.

I can hope, right?

CHAPTER 2
WOLF

Deciding not to stray too far from the bus, I take a good look at the people surrounding me. There are twenty-four of us, fifteen males and nine females, of all ages. The youngest one is a little girl next to the girl who looks perpetually annoyed.

"Does it look like Earth to you?!" I overhear from the crowd as a fifty-year-old man points toward the second, rather questionable sun. I can see spit flying out of his mouth and veins popping up on his forehead. "We can't just bloody sit here and wait for the police."

When he starts shouting, no one tries to calm him down, and it even appears that some of them agree with him. "We should look around first, maybe climb on some trees or something."

I can't help but roll my eyes as I stop listening to him.

We're surrounded by trees in all directions. They look ordinary. Like the trees you'd find on Earth...

I stop my thoughts.

Earth.

I think about it. Did I already determine that we aren't on Earth anymore?

It appears so.

After pondering for a bit longer, I come up with a few options, each more ludicrous than the last:

First, someone kidnapped us. Put us to sleep, perhaps with the help of some gas sedative filling up the bus. Afterward, they waited until morning and then let us wake up in the middle of the forest while somehow faking the second sun.

I find this option highly improbable as I don't remember falling asleep. Sure, I was sleepy, but I didn't fall asleep. The only thing I recall is a flash, us falling down together with the bus and then just being here. There are no empty spots in my memory, and I don't feel as if anything is missing.

Second, I am dead. The flash I saw was us crashing into something, maybe an explosion. Perhaps I got shot through the window. It would mean that this is some weird kind of afterlife.

I also find this option improbable, not to mention utterly depressing.

Third, I fell asleep, and this is a dream.

I pinch my forearm as hard as I can. The pain feels way too real, and I'm now mildly annoyed at myself.

Fourth, some kind of convoluted prank.

I think about it for a minute, and after I can't come up with a way they would pull it off or why they would even bother, I nearly dismiss it. It still lingers, though, because honestly, who knows what people are capable of these days? I once again look toward the passengers. They're still "discussing." I slowly glance over every one of them,

but no one looks high profile enough, important enough, or rich enough for such a waste of resources.

I don't completely scratch out this option, but it's also highly improbable.

Fifth, we really are on another planet.

The main reason is this bloody orange thing in the sky.

I just can't find anything fake about it. Not a single thing.

Of course, you would expect higher temperatures, but with the first sun looking slightly smaller and the second one looking weaker, it might balance out. I don't know, to be honest. My knowledge about this kind of stuff is pretty much just the basics.

I sigh.

Then I hear one of the schoolgirls screaming and pointing toward the forest. I follow the direction she is pointing toward and notice a wolf standing on the edge of the forest.

The beast's brown fur is matted with dried blood. It's missing an ear and bearing a gruesome scar on its snout. It fixes its unnerving gaze on the terrified girl, eyes glowing with an eerie light.

This massive creature is tall enough for its eyes to be at the same height as mine.

It takes a menacing step toward us—a huge, car-sized wolf with a strange text hovering above its head.

> **[Wolf - Level 2]**

Yeah, nope. I am out.

Thank you and fuck you, whoever is responsible for this monstrosity.

I make my way back inside the bus as the wolf moves toward us and lets out a deep, long growl. I can feel it in my chest. The deep, disturbing vibration and all my instincts scream at me to run.

Yup, it's definitely time to run.

Everyone runs and screams as they retreat to the bus, falling and crawling, and some men even pushing kids out of their way just to get in first.

The wolf slowly and carefully walks toward us. He almost seems like he is expecting some kind of trap, an inhuman intelligence shining in his eyes.

While not turning my back to him, I get to the bus and enter it as well. Everyone is already inside. I hear a few people sobbing, their voices scared.

"What the hell is that...?"

"...At least two meters tall."

"Level..."

While they are staring at the wolf, I look around, searching for something I could use as a weapon... I glance outside at...that thing.

Unsurprisingly, there is no weapon lying around. Hell, I would like an RPG at this point.

Fortunately, I notice a slightly bent iron pole used for people to hold on to, and after a little bit of pulling with all my force, I manage to free it. It's unfortunately only around a meter long and blunt. After another second, I grab a bigger piece of glass from the ground and hold it in my left hand while holding the pole in my right one.

Probably because of my nervousness or shaking hand, I can already see blood from my cut hand on the piece of glass, but I quickly ignore it.

The wolf is around ten meters away from the bus, looking even more dangerous than before. It is sniffing and growling while showing its massive teeth. It has lowered its body closer to the ground as if getting ready to attack or run. Its steps are slower and slower as it starts making circles around the bus while letting out horrifying growls.

"Hey, Google, what's the opposite of 'pspspsp,' but for wolves instead of cats?" the boy with the annoying laugh says, his voice shaking and his face pale as snow.

He gets a few shocked looks but no laughs. Everyone is looking absolutely terrified, and I am sure some people can't even see the wolf because of their tears.

"Mommy..."

"Oh my god, please let me..."

"G-get away from the windows..."

The wolf's circles are getting smaller and smaller, and it seems to be getting more and more comfortable.

My eyes are glued to the text over the wolf's head.

[Wolf – Level 2]

I look around, but I don't see anyone with such text over their head. I focus and try to filter out all the screams, cries, and wolf's growling. A crazy thought flashes through my mind.

It can't be, right?

"Profile," I whisper. Nothing happens.

"Character window," I say.

Nothing.

"Window," I say.

Nothing.

"Level," I say.

Nothing.

"Inspect," I say.

Nothing.

"Appraise," I say.

Nothing.

"Shut the fuck up with your mumbling!" one of the men yells at me.

"Shut the..." I start, but then I realize that a few people are watching me like I've gone crazy.

For a second, I look around. Some of the passengers already have some kind of "weapon" in their hands, like a glass bottle, a piece of glass from the window, a purse, a messenger bag, or another piece of iron pipe from the bus.

The wolf is two meters away from us, drool dripping from its massive maw.

"Skill window," I say.

Nothing.

"Skill," I say.

Nothing.

"Skills," I say.

Nothing.

"Status window," I say.

Nothing.

I hear screams and see the wolf's massive head behind one of the unbroken windows. Everyone is trying to get as far away as they can, shaking, screaming, and crying while waving their makeshift weapons and trying to look as dangerous as they can.

"Status," I say.

Before I have a chance to say another word, a golden see-through window pops up in front of my face.

[Name: Nathaniel Gwyn]
Difficulty: Hell
Floor: 1
Time left until forced return: 4y 364d 23h 36m 12s
Level: 0
Strength: 6
Dexterity: 7
Constitution: 3
Mana: 1
[Primary Class: Unavailable]
[Subclass: Unavailable]
Skills:
Focus - Level 1
Mana Manipulation - Level 1
[Skill Points: 0]
[Stat Points: 0]

Oh boy...this is interesting, but useless at the moment.

CHAPTER 3
FOCUS

The window disappears when it decides to do so, and then the bus's window breaks, and the wolf sticks its head inside, ignoring the broken glass and trying to bite a nearby older woman. The wolf manages to latch on to her sweater, but as the fabric tears, its teeth graze her arm, drawing blood. It tries to yank her outside, and the woman falls to the ground, screaming loudly, holding her wounded arm.

I move slightly to the side, holding an iron pipe and a piece of glass in my hand. Then I notice a man on the opposite side of the wolf, reaching under his jacket, toward his armpit.

Don't tell me...

I step a bit closer to the wolf, and its eyes turn toward me. It shifts its head slightly, totally ignoring the broken glass. Its eyes are almost glowing.

As I get its attention, the man pulls out a pistol, and for a second, our gazes meet. I give him a little nod and step a bit closer to the wolf.

I am standing just a meter or two away from the wolf, and I feel my heart race. My muscles feel warmed up, my heart aggressively circulates blood in my veins, and my mind clears.

There is only me, the wolf, and the man with the gun. I don't hear screams anymore, nor do I feel pain from my pinched forearm or cut palm. I squeeze the piece of glass.

How long has it been since I felt so alive?

Did I ever feel so alive?

[Focus - Level 1 > Focus - Level 2]

I feel the corners of my lips lifting up slightly as I lower my body, calculating how far the wolf can reach and how fast it was before. Just to be sure, I add some amount to its reach and double its speed.

I can feel my muscles squeezing and exploding as I lunge toward the wolf.

It looks almost as if it is smiling as it opens its big mouth—teeth as big as the palm of my hand.

I stop just in time, and its mouth snaps shut just a few centimeters away from me.

Realizing my terrible miscalculation, I add more to its speed and reach in my mind. I move my right hand and try to stab the blunt piece of iron pipe into its ear while predicting the wolf's dodge.

The pipe hits its eyebrow, and the wolf lets out a deep growl and instantly attacks again.

But I am not there anymore.

This time, its maw snaps a bit further from me, and I slash with my left hand, slicing its upper lip slightly.

I jump back, and the wolf keeps trying to push its head toward me. The iron plates of the bus creak and groan.

Finally, I hear five quick and loud explosions. Inside the bus, they are deafening, and for the first time, the wolf lets out a loud cry, quickly pulling its head outside. I hear two more shots, and the wolf jumps backward. I notice a slight limping as it does so, and it cries once again.

It looks wounded, but not fatally.

It starts slowly walking backward with its attention turned toward the guy with the handgun. I can see blood dripping down the wolf's face. It looks like a few bullets hit the right side of its face and some of its legs.

My gaze once again moves toward the text above its head.

[Wolf - Level 2]

The monstrous wolf is slowly moving toward the forest when I make my decision.

"Screw it."

I put the glass and pole on the seat next to me and quickly pull off my shirt. I tie the shirt around my left hand and grab the piece of glass once again. This time, my grip is stronger without the glass cutting into my palm.

I lodge the tip of the pipe under the seat and try pulling and pushing it. When I get it out, I step on it a few times with my full force, trying to sharpen the tip of it at least a little bit.

My breathing is heavy, and I can hear my blood pumping in my ears.

The wolf is already near the forest, slowly turning around when I jump out of the window and dash toward it—bare-chested, dirty, and holding my makeshift weapons.

Shaking.

Scared.

Intoxicated.

The wolf turns toward me, and my mind is clearer than ever before.

I slow down, walking while lowering my body, and the monster lets out a deep growl. I decide not to lower its speed in my mind. Underestimating him could be a big mistake.

It is bleeding and looks weaker, but I decide not to underestimate the monster. Sure. I wouldn't go after it if it didn't get shot and wasn't heavily injured, but this isn't an animal from Earth.

If it's like I think, we can level up if we kill such monsters. Get skills, get stats. Become stronger, and survive until the forced-return activates.

Just like a game. A goddamn game.

I know I am risking my life here, but I don't think I will get a much better chance than now. If the wolf dies, it will probably count as if the guy with the handgun killed it, so I have to damage it at least a little bit and hope it will do something. It might survive, and then not even the guy with the gun will get anything. In the worst-case scenario, it will come back with more wolves.

On Earth, wolves are social creatures.

The wolf slowly moves toward me, and I start moving to the left, the side where it got shot. Slowly, carefully.

My senses feel sharp. I am not even blinking as I watch the wolf's legs and shoulders, waiting for it to telegraph its next move.

Here.

I quickly sidestep to the left and then once more, thrusting with my left hand to try to stab its eye with the piece of glass. It's just a glancing blow, but it leaves a deep wound over its eye.

The wolf instantly turns around, trying to bite me, but I am already moving backward and swinging with my right hand, hitting its nose.

The wolf quickly attacks again, and this time, I move to the right and slash once again, trying to hit its left eye. I connect, and with a loud cry, the wolf jumps backward—a piece of glass lodged into its left eye.

I bend my knees and dash slightly to the left, and while grabbing the pipe with both of my hands, I hit its left eye, destroying the shard of glass and injuring it even further. I dodge its next attack to the left, its blind side, and as forceful as I can, I hit its blinded eye once again.

The wolf lets out a painful cry, some of its blood splashing on me.

It jumps backward, but I dash once more. My body feels strong and light. My hands aren't shaking anymore, and I feel like I can't see anything else but the wolf. Its movements, twitching muscles, telegraphing its motions. Its paws burrow into the ground as it prepares its attack.

I stab the wolf's blinded eye with the tip of the pipe and jump back.

My body feels like it's burning, and my heart is beating like crazy. I try to gulp, but my throat is parched.

I slowly take a deep breath.

I don't think I am going to lose. The wolf is stronger, faster, and much more resilient. But I don't think I will lose.

I dash, but this time toward its right side. The wolf attacks the opposite side, probably expecting me to attack its blinded eye once again, but instead of that, I lift the pipe over my head, and with all the strength I can muster, I hit its left eye.

It's not blinded, but there is blood flowing from a deep wound over the eye, partially blocking its vision.

The hit connects, and as a few times before, the wolf cries and jumps back.

Expecting that, I am already dashing toward its right side and hitting it once again, finally blinding its other eye.

I stop.

While the wolf thrashes around, biting toward all sides, I take a deep breath.

Calm down.

Focus.

I breathe out.

Focus.

[Focus – Level 2 > Focus – Level 3]

I take a deep, slow breath, calming down my rapidly beating heart. My body feels like it's burning, and my muscles ache. I'm lightheaded, and there is a deep scratch on the left side of my chest. I didn't even notice it. I look at the wound, slightly surprised.

The wolf stops attacking and starts letting out quiet cries while shifting and baring its teeth.

While untying the shirt from my left hand, I move toward its right side. I make a ball from my bloodied shirt

and throw it to the right. After waiting for a second, I dash toward the left side while grabbing the pipe with both hands and pointing the slightly sharpened side toward the ground.

The monster jumps toward the shirt, letting out a horrifying noise as it bites.

While trying to stay as quiet as I can, I lift my hands high in the air and thrust downward with the pipe in my hands, aiming for the wolf's left eye.

The monster wolf cries as I push the pipe as deep into the eye as I can before letting go and jumping away from it. I watch the wolf thrashing around while growling, biting, and dashing in random directions.

I grab my shirt from the ground and start walking back to the bus while not taking my eyes off the wolf. It sniffs and then limps toward the forest while growling. The monster hits one tree but ignores it and enters deeper into the forest with the steel pipe still lodged in its eye. The world slowly comes back into focus as the wolf disappears, and I can hear the people from inside the bus.

Pain hits me in waves. My wounds. My burning muscles. My head feels like it's about to explode.

Out of nowhere, I lose the strength in my legs, almost falling to my knees. Only my will keeps me standing.

My heartbeat slows down, and the world... The world feels ordinary again, once more.

CHAPTER 4
MANIPULATION

When I turn around, I see a few people getting out of the bus. The man with a handgun is one of them.

"I've never seen such a dumbass in my life," he said and shook his head.

I just nod, totally agreeing with him. I try to force a smile on my face, but it doesn't work.

"No, I am not suicidal," I answer one guy. Isn't it kind of rude to ask something like that?

"Yes, it was dumb," I answer an older lady. What are you, my mom?

"Yes, it hurts a lot." No shit.

"I just thought I had to." Let's act like a good little boy. Blah, blah.

I just try to force out answers people want to hear and look as normal and harmless as possible. I am guessing we won't be coming back to Earth anytime soon, so it isn't bad to try to make some "friends." I can't just sleep with

my eyes open, and there might be things other people are better at than me.

After a few minutes of questioning, I start feeling uncomfortable with people surrounding me and asking questions. My energy drops even more than after a fight with a wolf.

I know I'm not particularly social, but I try not to let it be too obvious, so I answer a few more questions, give a few pieces of advice, and then tell them about "status." That finally makes them shut up, and they just stare into the air a few centimeters in front of their face. As I thought, their windows are invisible to me.

I sneak away to the opposite side of the bus and sit down on the grass, resting my back against the tire.

Who knew that even in another world, surrounded by monsters, the most dangerous beings are extroverts?

A few minutes later, I feel much better without people surrounding me.

I slowly lift my shirt from my side, dried blood slightly gluing it to the wound. Fortunately, I am not bleeding anymore, and the wound doesn't seem as bad as I thought.

A sigh leaves my mouth as I put the shirt back on my wound. It could be worse. Much worse. I should be able to find a first aid kit on the bus, but there is something more important now.

What the hell was that?

I am not even talking about the giant wolf, nor about two suns in the sky, or these goddamn holographic windows with text over the wolf's head.

I am sure I can adapt and survive it. As always.

But...

Once my decision-making goes the wrong way, I am dead.

So why did I do that? I close my eyes and reflect on my actions.

Sure, I did feel some boredom back on Earth. Lack of excitement or change. Something to strive for. But that doesn't sound like a good enough reason to charge a gigantic wolf.

It's not me. I don't act like that. I know myself well enough to say it with certainty. So let's think about it.

Could it be some kind of mind manipulation? Is someone controlling my feelings or at least giving me impulses to charge at the wolf? I already noticed two new skills in my "status," and I am more than sure that there are many others.

I look at the people around the bus. One of them? I did get two skills at the start, so what if I try to replay the whole fight in my head from the start to the end?

At first, I just wanted to get the wolf's attention so the guy could shoot it. That feels like something I would do as it's helpful for my survival and not too risky. During that part of the fight, I felt strength filling my body as I increased my focus. I felt as if I could control my body to an unusual degree. I bet that's the skill called Focus. More testing is needed, but I am pretty sure of that.

It's possible that someone manipulated me during the fight. I have no way of knowing if it was just something like sending me some impulse to fight longer in hopes of killing the wolf or someone unable to control their skill. Some scared passenger sent me to my death.

Another option is for them to realize the skills they have and use them on me while not caring if I die or live. That also sounds plausible.

Then there is also a chance that it was something the wolf did, but looking at how he ended up...

I sigh and look at the sky. I need more information, testing, and time.

For now, it will be best to watch my feelings and impulses. One mistake can lead to my death, so I would rather think twice and analyze everything I do.

I will find the responsible person, and if I can't use them, I will have to deal with them.

Yes, let's do that. My mind is mine and mine only.

I feel anger rising up deep from inside me, the anger I pushed to the back of my mind. This time, I didn't even bother to think if this impulse is me or someone manipulating my feelings.

Chapter 5
Level One

[You have defeated a Wolf - Level 2]
[Level 0 > Level 1]

After resting against the tire of the bus for a few minutes, I receive a message indicating that the wolf had finally died. Either it succumbed to its wounds, or another animal finished it off. Well, at least I got enough experience to level up.

[Name: Nathaniel Gwyn]
Difficulty: Hell
Floor: 1
Time left until forced return: 4y 364d 23h 12m 3s
Level: 1
Strength: 6
Dexterity: 8
Constitution: 3
Mana: 2

[Primary Class: Unavailable]
[Subclass: Unavailable]
Skills:
Focus - Level 3
Mana Manipulation - Level 1
[Skill Points: 0]
[Stat Points: 3]

I got three stat points, and my level changed. Also, somehow my Mana and Dexterity went up by one point each.

One hour. I can't believe we have been here for such a short time. I try touching the holographic window with my finger, but nothing happens. My finger just passes through.

"Stat explanation."

Nothing.

Not again. I am too tired for this. I'm sure there will be some gamers on the bus, so I can make them do all the work, but for now, there is one stat I can't go wrong with.

"Put one stat point into constitution," I try, and one stat point disappears. Huh? It actually worked.

Now I try to focus and think about wanting to put a single stat point into constitution. It takes a moment, but then I get a feeling as if someone is asking me for confirmation, but in my mind. It's unsettling, but I send back something like a thought version of "yes," and another point disappears. This could be useful.

I quickly add the last remaining point into constitution and close the status window.

Now back to stats.

Strength and Dexterity should be self-explanatory, and constitution should be something like endurance, vitality,

health, or an all-in-one stat. Hopefully, it will help me heal faster or require less rest.

There is no need to be greedy for power or speed. As I already noticed, I can level up my stats even without stat points, and survival is most important at the moment. I don't know if it's the placebo effect, but I already feel better. Well, let's wait and find out.

Now, mana. I already used mana to strengthen my body. I think.

The movement I showed while fighting the wolf should have been impossible for me. It could be Focus, Mana Manipulation, or both. If I learn how to control it, it will increase my chances of survival.

Okay, I will figure it out later.

My name. Somehow, the system knows my real name. The best thing I can do at the moment is to be prepared not to be surprised if some of my private information pops up out of nowhere.

Freezing from the surprise in the middle of a dangerous situation can be deadly, so for now, let's think that the entity controlling the system knows everything about me. While we are here, I need to let go of my life on Earth and focus on surviving here.

It might be pretty drastic, but I am at the mercy of the entity, system, and the only sensible thing is to focus on surviving. It's better to think that I will be stranded here for five more years, and that's long enough for people to declare us dead.

Let's forget about everyone on Earth—my mother, my sister, everyone. There will be time to grieve or celebrate after I get forcibly returned, so it's better to be pleasantly surprised than any other option.

Well, it's not like there are that many people I care about. To be honest, the list may be really short.

The most important thing at the moment is my survival, and I can't let anything distract me.

Let's use other passengers as well. I should act fairly friendly but distant enough. At the same time, I can't let them use me. I need to act a bit more distant. I can also put on a strong front. If I set it up right, it will be a nice combination of give and take, with me taking more than giving.

For a second, a thought flashes through my mind—would it be possible to level up by killing them? Oh boy, this is getting dark. Still, I give it some thought. I started with Level 0, and others are most likely the same. Even if it's possible to level up by killing people, I am Level 1 at the moment, and I would most likely need to kill most of them. If it's even possible to gain experience from Level 0 or a human.

It might even be on purpose that everyone is Level 0.

Also, I already decided on using them—well, at least from the start and until I collect more data or become stronger, so let's not go this way.

Sounds good.

I take the shirt off my chest, and I don't know if it's just me, but the wound already looks better.

Another thing from the status is the word "forced" return. If I had to say, it means that there is a way to return to Earth without waiting for five years. Not a forced way of returning.

But...do I even want to?

Well, probably yes, as it's much safer that way, however...

Later...I will reflect on that later.

The "Floor 1" part in the status is interesting as well. It means there are more floors, and if I think about it as a game, we will have to fill out some requirements to move to a lower or upper floor, or we will be moved there after some time. Maybe after five years? That doesn't sound right—we never went to another floor, so we don't have any place to return to. The only fitting place to return to is Earth.

Let's collect more info first and then think about it again.

The difficulty is pretty disturbing—Hell.

In games, the difficulties are usually categorized as easy, normal, and hard, with "hell" sometimes representing the most challenging level. Therefore, I must be extremely cautious. When facing an enemy, I need to make sure not to underestimate them, even if they appear weaker.

I am also curious about why I got this difficulty, which may be the hardest one, but at the moment, I have no way of finding out. There is also the possibility that there is an even harder difficulty, but no way of confirming it at the moment, or at least I don't know about any.

Classes sound interesting, but I don't have the option to pick one. There may be special requirements, or I need to level up more.

It is already clear that the system knows a lot about me, and it's highly possible that I am being watched by it even at the moment. It doesn't even have to be someone personally watching over me, just some kind of program writing down my actions and thoughts.

Now when I think about it, even the process of leveling up is kind of weird. I have an idea of how it works in games, but being stuck in this situation makes me want to think about it a bit more logically.

There is a possibility that leveling up is just a reward from the entity/system for killing the monster, which means that I was granted stat points by it after fulfilling the requirements of leveling up.

Taking a deep breath, I slowly stand up, but fortunately, my head doesn't spin.

It's time to socialize and find someone useful.

Chapter 6
The Gun

What welcomes me inside the bus is a bunch of people calmly discussing the situation we are in.

"Fuck you, I will not go into that goddamn forest! You go there if you want to die that much!"

Really calmly discussing the situation we're in... It looks like the wolf scared them, as all of them are inside the bus despite lack of air-conditioning turning it into a sauna.

Someone shouts out what I am thinking. "Sounds good, so just sit there and eat the grass. Maybe you can drink the gasoline as well."

Yes, water and food will be a problem. It's only been around an hour since we arrived, but I already feel thirsty and hungry, most likely because of the energy I used.

Even if they are not hungry at the moment and have a bottle of water with them or a little bit of food, soon they will need to look for more.

"So you're back." The man with the gun approaches me and falls silent for a moment, watching the bus driver conversing with two men. "You good?"

I nod. I have already put my white shirt on. Ahem, my *formerly* white shirt. I guess it's red now.

"We will need some water and maybe food, and it would be best if we look for it before sunset," he says directly.

He seems to be on the calm side, and from the way he watches other people, I can say that he is in a better state than most others. Anyway, he should have a good impression of me as well. Hopefully. Well, maybe not that good. In his eyes, I might be a suicidal lunatic.

He looks at me for a whole minute with a deep, discerning stare, as if he's trying to see inside my head.

His stare makes me slightly nervous, especially knowing that he should have leveled up as well. Who knows what skills he got or how he will use his stat points?

I break the silence. "So how many bullets do you have left?"

He once again falls silent and looks at me, a slight smile slowly appearing on his face.

"Not too many." There is a hint of amusement and warmth in his voice.

"I see."

He was careful and not too trusting.

He is slightly shorter than me. His figure is pretty robust and muscular, with a sense of authority around him. It might be caused by his gun, but I don't believe that's just it.

A cop? Maybe.

"Nathaniel." I reach out my hand to him, and he accepts. His grip is strong, and he looks into my eyes while shaking my hand. Like I do to him, he is also judging me.

"Hadwin," he says.

I notice a few people staring at us, but I ignore them for now.

"Did you also level up?"

"Yes." The bus quiets down, and I can see them listening to us. "I already used my stat points. One of the kids told me to do so." He nods toward the school kids. "It's crazy when you think about it. Us appearing in the middle of nowhere, two suns, gigantic wolf..." He smiles awkwardly while looking around.

When he looks back at me, his smile is gone.

"You know," he starts, and I can see that he is trying to find the right words. "I thought about it, and I think we should look around. We will need water soon, and we might find out something about this place."

I can tell what's going to be next.

"Do you want to join me?" His eyes seem honest and firm as he asks me to risk my life.

So shameless.

"Sure, let's go."

He slowly brushes his hair off his forehead, and his muscles tense a little bit. After a few seconds, he relaxes his body, and a quiet sigh escapes from his mouth.

"To be honest, I pretty much expected you to decline," he says.

"I gave it some thought." I shrug my shoulders. "We should look around while we are not starved or dehydrated. Logically, it will be harder the later we go."

"It's not about logic... People don't tend to think logically in situations like this..." Another sigh escapes from his mouth.

I feel like I should be insulted, but I let it go. I kind of like the way this goes. Let's put it all on Hadwin.

Yup. I like it.

"Others should keep watch while we look around."
He quickly gives a few orders, and I can see that he has
already talked to a few people, and they seem to respect
him enough to follow his orders.

I bet it is because of the gun.

Obviously, some of them seem dissatisfied with the
guy with a gun leaving them to go into the forest, but no
one says anything. Most likely, they are scared that he will
ask them to go with him.

I am not too surprised at their lack of initiative. It's
weirder that Hadwin and I plan to go there without being
pressured to do so.

Hadwin grabs his backpack and two iron pipes, clearly
inspired by me. He gives me one, and I take it.

Some of the passengers see it and start talking amongst
themselves, and I see some of them trying to pry out their
own pipes.

What's with that reaction time? As we are about to
leave the bus, someone stops us.

"Do you have a spot?"

On the bus, there are a few men, and the one asking is
one of them. He is close to two meters in height and slim,
but his shoulders are surprisingly broad. His face is on the
handsome side, and he is smoothly shaven.

"Maybe..." Hadwin stops next to me.

"Damon." He reaches his hand toward Hadwin and
then me.

Hadwin's shake was just a greeting, but Damon's is
clearly some sort of test as he squeezes my hand as strongly
as he can. As he lets go of my hand, his gaze stays on me a
bit longer than on Hadwin.

"I would like to join you. I grew up in the countryside,
so I shouldn't be baggage inside the forest."

That almost makes me smile, as if something like that would help wherever we are. But, well, in the worst case, we can use him as bait. Something tells me that Hadwin wouldn't like it, but I can work around it.

"Sounds good," says Hadwin, and I just nod. Damon once again looks into my eyes.

Look at him. I feel amused as his look isn't too friendly—more like the opposite.

As we exit the bus, no one else joins us. No one is brave or desperate enough to come with us. Not yet.

Well, almost no one. I saw one of the school kids wanting to join us, but others stopped him. Well, I call them kids, but all of them are around eighteen years old, not that much younger than me.

Bless you, kid. Maybe next time?

After something eats Damon.

CHAPTER 7
FOREST

Outside, we find the annoyed girl leaning against the bus. She is clearly keeping watch, looking toward the place where the wolf came from.

It's a good idea.

She is around my height, slim, and has an athletic figure. The most striking thing about her is her deep green eyes, which are even more noticeable against her tanned skin and black hair.

"I want to join you," she says without holding back. Her voice shakes almost unnoticeably as she says so, yet she seems determined. "I need to level up."

Oh? Did they have a group talk inside the bus while I was thinking outside? They seem fairly used to the idea of leveling up.

"I need to become stronger as soon as possible. Wolves usually don't move alone, and...we don't know what else is here. I swear I won't slow you down."

Everyone should be Level 0, with only Hadwin and me being higher level, so she also might be worried to lag behind us. Or does she just want to protect the little girl next to her?

Did Hadwin share the results with others? Did he put all three points into strength and test it out while they were watching?

How much of a difference would three points make?

"I don't think we have to worry about that," says Hadwin, to my surprise. "The wolf from before did look starved and wounded, and he didn't even try to call for other wolves before attacking us." He looks at us. "So it's either the last surviving wolf from the pack, or they chased him away from it."

I like the sound of that. I really do but...

"I think we should expect the worst option," I say as their eyes turn to me. I shrug and don't say more.

"I partly agree with you," Hadwin says carefully, caressing his short beard as he speaks. "But we shouldn't let it scare us too much. Doing nothing because we are too worried could cost us."

I'm slightly disappointed. He seems too confident. Whatever. If it seems like he's too careless, I can leave them.

"Hadwin." As he extends his hand, the black-haired girl grabs it. "I have to warn you. It will be really dangerous out there."

She just nods and shakes his hand.

"Sophie."

"Damon."

"Nathaniel," I add, and for a second, our eyes meet.

"I know," she says very quietly. Hadwin and Damon probably didn't hear it, but I could because she is standing a little bit closer to me.

I try to think about it, but I can't remember her at all. Maybe I met her at the gym? She seems fairly athletic, and there aren't that many places where she could meet me. It could be said that I avoided human interaction like the plague.

I look at the girl next to her, who's stayed quiet up until now. She looks similar to Sophie, not as tanned, but her hair is the same, and her eyes are a slightly lighter shade of green. She is around ten years old, but it's hard for me to tell.

She is also shyly half-hiding behind Sophie, peeking with big and wide-open eyes.

That can be a problem.

"I hope you don't plan to take a kid with you." As expected, Damon sounds as annoying as he looks.

It's not like I don't agree with him—quite the opposite. There is no way we are going to take a little kid with us. Damon just sounds...super punchable.

"I am not..." It's clear that Sophie wants to go with us, but at the same time, where should she leave the little kid? With whom?

The girl slightly pulls the shirt of a distressed Sophie, and she turns to her with a smile on her face. To me, it looks fake, but I guess it's good enough to trick a little girl.

"Don't worry, Izzy." She gently caresses her head, and there is a lot of gentleness and love in her action.

However hard this might be, I am glad I ended up here alone.

"How about you leave her with Jacob? He seems like a good guy," Hadwin finally says. "She will be safer with others." He pauses. "You can stay too...with your..."

"Sister..." Sophie says slowly.

"Sister." Hadwin kneels in front of the girl, and a big, soft smile appears on his face. "God knows I would do the same."

The little girl proceeds to avoid his gaze and looks back up at Sophie.

I think it's already taking too long. She is most likely scared of being left behind and probably not trusting us that much either. Who knows what would happen if we came back much stronger?

For now, it looks like nothing much has changed, but the moment some of us obtain strength way beyond others, things will become...difficult.

"You should come," I say as Sophie turns toward me with a surprised look on her face. Her sister starts peeking again. "We most likely won't go too far at first. Not far enough to not hear if something happens."

It's obvious that she already decided to go with us, so why is she struggling that much? Just trust your own decisions and then take responsibility if something happens.

"One or two hours should be enough to scan our closest surroundings. After that, we will come back with some wood, which we can use for weapons and fire," I suggest. "If something happens, they can use the bus horn, and we can rush back as quickly as possible."

After a little while, she finally accepts the plan and disappears inside the bus with her sister. I can see her talking to the bus guy, Jacob, apparently. Her sister starts crying.

"For fuck's sake," Damon complains.

When Sophie comes back, we finally start walking toward the forest. Not coincidentally, we walk on the opposite side of where the wolf came from. Everyone stops talking as we come closer to the trees, and the atmosphere instantly changes. It's as if the closer we get to the trees, the more nervous everyone becomes.

Interestingly enough, the trees seem normal.

Tree branches wave slightly as the suns shine through the crowns of the trees.

I don't know what I expected. Shining leaves? Faces on trunks? Whispers in the wind?

CHAPTER 8
GOBLINS

I keep my guard up as we enter the forest and squeeze the iron pipe in my hand. For a start, let's not touch anything. Who knows what's poisonous?

Hadwin enters first, closely followed by us. His iron pipe is behind his belt, and there is the gun in his hands. I am not an expert, but the way he holds it seems like someone that is used to weapons.

Maybe he really is a policeman. Judging from the way he talks and acts, I wouldn't be surprised.

"Focus and listen to our surroundings," he says as he slowly walks between the trees. "Nathaniel, you will take my left, Damon, you focus on your right, and Sophie, you will have our back."

I slightly change my position. Obviously, I don't focus only on the left, but I give it a bit more focus than other directions. Don't forget to check the tops of the trees as well.

"Whisper, and if you hear flowing water, see wet places, puddles, or anything suspicious, let us know."

We slowly continue. It's almost funny. A bunch of adults led by a dangerous-looking man armed with a handgun sneaking through a normal-looking forest.

Fortunately, the forest isn't too dense, so we move without a problem.

Thirty minutes later, I hear Damon cursing under his breath.

"Motherfucking alien forest."

I don't blame him. Every one of us twitches every time we hear the slightest noise. After a while, it's really tiring. We continue as Hadwin leads us in a circle around the clearing with a bus. The clearing is on our right side, and we didn't walk too deep inside the forest.

I also noted that Damon touched the trees a few times, and he looks fine, so they most likely aren't poisonous.

"We are getting to the place where the wolf came from," Hadwin says.

Just this sentence is enough to bring us to the tips of our toes. Damon instantly shuts up, and I can almost hear him squeezing his weapon.

Somehow, I feel calmer than before.

"Movement to our left," I whisper, and I hear Hadwin's gun click as he turns it toward his left. "A bit more to your right."

I squeeze the pipe in my hand as two human-like beings rush at us at once, holding primitive weapons in their hands.

I step to the left and avoid a stab with a spear. They don't seem to be too tall, almost like kids or young adults, so I hesitate.

Then I hear a gunshot, just one, followed by a weird scream.

I dodge another stab and swing with the pipe, it connects, and I hit the creature's head.

Its head is harder than expected, so I hit once more while using as much strength as I can while dodging its aggressive but clumsy stab. The creature falls down.

When I look around, Hadwin is already running after another one.

[Goblin - Level 3]

The goblin is shot, and Hadwin is holding the pipe in his hands, closely behind the monster.

Sophie and Damon are fighting the third enemy, which surprisingly attacked from somewhere behind us.

[Goblin - Level 2]

Another Level 2. They seem to be overpowering it, especially Sophie, with some clearly well-trained moves.

Not bothering to help them, I quickly follow Hadwin. I am sure he wants to stop the goblin from running away and maybe bringing back more of them, but at the same time, he is saving his bullets.

I quickly find him fighting the monster. The green creature seems to be mortally wounded by his gun, so that makes it easier.

While slowing down to walk, I keep my eyes on Hadwin. His movements are careful and calculating as he slowly makes a half-circle around the creature, which is swinging something that looks like a knife.

There are wounds other than gunshots covering the creature's body. It seems like the older man did get in some attacks. Out of nowhere, the cornered creature quickly dashes at him, but its movements are just that— quick. There is no technique and no other intent than just violence.

Hadwin almost dodges it, but the creature hits him with the edge of its shoulder, making him lose his balance and fall down. For its size, the green monster is surprisingly strong.

I am already on my way as it starts a downward stab, and Hadwin lifts up the pipe against it. Before it connects, I hit the creature's hand with my full strength, making its knife fall as it screams.

The goblin turns toward me, a murderous look in its red eyes. I can see its pointy teeth as it fully opens its mouth and rushes at me with a loud scream. In one move, I dodge to the right and hit the back of its head as inertia makes the goblin move forward.

Of course, it's not enough, and the goblin charges me again. This time, I dodge to the left and follow up with a kick, focusing more on pushing it further away than on damaging it.

The goblin screams with rage and turns back to me as I pick up its knife from the ground.

For a second, it makes a beautifully dumbfounded look.

One long and quick step.

Stab.

It puts its hands in front of its neck. But in the middle of the move, I change the direction of the stab, and the knife easily enters its eye.

I step back just far enough to dodge the blindly waving hand.

Surprisingly still alive, the creature screams and scratches its face.

Then Hadwin hits its temple from the side. The goblin falls to the ground. The second hit from Hadwin lands as the goblin starts twitching. Last hit. I can hear the wet and nauseating noise of the iron pipe breaking its skull.

The goblin finally stops screaming.

[You have defeated a Goblin - Level 3]

Then I notice my wildly shaking hand, tense muscles, and rough breathing. The world comes back into focus.

Hadwin is breathing heavily and cursing.

I hear Sophie and Damon not far away from us.

"One goblin is only unconscious. Can you keep a watch?"

Hadwin nods with a tired imitation of a smile, and I can see the sweat running down his forehead.

Before running back, I grab the knife and pull it out of the goblin's eye. It makes a disgusting noise I am sure I will remember for a while.

When I get back to Sophie and Damon, I can see them repeatedly hitting the goblin they were fighting against. It seems to be dead, but they don't stop.

They have furious looks on their faces, and I can see some wounds on their bodies, painful yet not serious. The goblin I stunned is still lying on the ground. I kick its leg while standing as far away as possible, and when it doesn't react, I calm down slightly.

I still can feel the adrenaline flowing through me and probably mana as well, and just now, I am slowly realizing what happened, as if I am coming back to reality.

My heart is beating wildly, and multiple feelings wash over my body.

Fear, relief...desperation.

Calm down.

Think logically.

Calm down.

Focus.

My breathing slows, I finally catch my breath, and my focus comes back to normal.

I am such a mess.

I hear quiet sobs from Sophie behind me, but she quickly stops, almost choking on them.

While clenching my teeth, I slowly lower my body carefully while watching the unconscious goblin. And then, without hesitation, I stab a dagger deep into its eye.

> **[You have defeated a Goblin – Level 2]**
> **[Level 1 > Level 2]**

CHAPTER 9
WE SHOULD DISSECT THEM

I decide to ignore stat points for now as I want to test their effects a bit more. I pull the dagger out of the goblin's eye.

Damon and Sophie seem to be shaken. Damon is naturally athletic and strong, with long limbs, meaning his reach is pretty big. Sophie seems to be well-versed in martial arts, but even so, this creature, around a meter and a half tall, managed to hurt them in a two-vs.-one fight.

"Asshole..." Damon kicks the goblin's corpse.

It just seems like a way of hiding his fear. I can even see his shaking hands and hear a slight tremble in his voice.

"Can you carry its corpse?"

He looks at me like I'm crazy.

"There might be more of them, and we don't want them to find their friends' corpses," I add before he says anything.

He just nods solemnly after a short pause.

"Sophie," I say, and she looks up.

Oh. I like the look in her eyes.

"I'll carry the other one, and you can help Hadwin," she says.

She catches on pretty fast.

"Carry only the corpses; Hadwin or I will take care of the rest." I pause. "Don't bring them too close to other passengers for now."

She nods.

I go deeper into the forest. The dagger is once again in my hand. It's made out of some kind of obsidian-like stone, but it's surprisingly sharp and hard.

Hadwin is looking at the corpse of the goblin, and I step next to him.

"Damon and Sophie will carry the other two away. I will take this one. Can you take care of their weapons?"

He nods. "I can also try to cover up some of our and their tracks."

"Sounds good."

To be honest, I partially expected something like that from Hadwin, but I wasn't so sure. I scan the man in front of me once again. Let's be a bit more careful with him.

The way he starts looking around and taking care of tracks that he can cover looks experienced to me, but I don't know much about bushcraft, so he could very well be making it worse.

I keep a watch while he does so, and when he is done with our closest surroundings, I kneel to lift up the goblin and put him over my shoulders.

Unintentionally, I let out a surprised noise as the goblin is much heavier than I expected him to be, probably around the weight of an adult man.

Goddamn green asshole.

For someone at this height, it's a lot, and he isn't even that bulky. But I guess we can't use human standards here.

Hadwin picks up the goblin's weapon and our stuff. My loyal pipe is there as well.

When we reach the spot where the fight started, Hadwin starts covering tracks or digging out ants or whatever he does. He is an expert here, not me.

Both goblins are gone, and in the end, Hadwin also grabs their weapons from the ground and watches our backs as I lead the way. The pistol is in his hand. The weapons and our stuff are under his other hand or inside his backpack.

We move quickly and quietly without a word, and once in a while, Hadwin does something that I guess is covering our tracks and those of our two companions.

After around fifteen minutes of walking, we reach the clearing.

I notice that I am not as tired as I should be after carrying such weight. Sure, I've lifted heavier weights before, but carrying it through the forest?

It's either adrenaline or, and I guess the more probable option, the effect of putting three stat points into constitution.

We find Damon and Sophie lying on the ground, breathing heavily, and covered in sweat. Their baggage is a few meters away from them, and the other passengers are surrounding the dead goblins.

Once again, I realize how much of a better state I'm in as I throw the green creature on the ground.

Damon has an angry look on his face as he turns to me. I don't say anything, just look back at him.

"Screw off," he breathes out and turns toward Hadwin.

"What the hell was that? What are these green little jerks?"

"Goblins."

"No shit. I asked—"

Before he can continue, the older man interrupts him. "I don't know, Damon. As you know, I've been here as long as you have." There is a slight frown on his face. "What I know is that we should be thankful that we are still alive. These...creatures are far stronger than they should be."

"And much heavier," Sophie says quietly. There is a questioning look on Hadwin's face. "The one I carried must have weighed more than me, and it's the smallest and slimmest one."

"Fucking hell, mine is for sure twice as heavy," Damon adds.

From the corner of my vision, I see Sophie roll her eyes.

Hadwin slowly walks toward my goblin and tries to lift him. Surprise appears on his face, but with a groan, he lifts him up.

"For sure, they are heavy," he says and puts him back on the ground.

Everyone falls silent.

"We should dissect them," I say after a while.

Their gaze instantly turns back to me. *Uhm? Why are you looking at me like that?*

Chapter 10
Curiosity

I had hoped that Hadwin would suggest it first, but I can see that he is holding back a little bit, still not fully realizing the situation we are in. Still not prepared to do everything it takes for his survival.

When they look at me with shocked looks in their eyes, I just shrug. I notice that only Hadwin appears somewhat relieved.

"You don't have to be there."

"I will help you," he says. "But we should do it far away from the clearing."

I stop to think about it for a second. Doing it here doesn't sound like a good idea. We don't know if blood will lure more monsters to us, and we don't know how the other passengers will react to it.

Well, I am sure that they will get used to it fairly soon.

"We have to get rid of them anyway. So let's just throw them out, and while doing so, I will quickly check a few things."

"There is no way I am going to carry that green little shit again," I hear Damon say, but everyone ignores him.

"Are you sure it's worth it?" Hadwin is still worried. "We will be taking a big risk."

While in deep thought, I look at the dead goblin. The words over his head are gone. Knowing that the text disappears when a monster dies helps.

The goblin is around Sophie's little sister's height—with a short torso but long legs and hands. Even though his limbs are slim, I remember their weight. He was also illogically stronger than his body appeared.

I lean over him and poke him with the tip of my finger. His skin feels thick, somewhat firmer than mine.

I pinch him, and I once again notice the firmness of his skin. Could it be his thicker skin adding to his weight?

The green creature is wearing some sort of primitive leather clothes covering parts where reproductive organs on humans would be. There are also light blue markings all over his body. When I glance at the other two goblins, I notice that they have similar markings. I try to rub them, but nothing stays on my finger. When I spit a little bit on it and try again, the result is the same.

Tattoo? Some kind of group, clan, or village marking?

I pause for a second, done thinking about it.

Okay, no dissecting. Let's just test a few things.

I pull out the knife I took from him and point the tip at his chest. I am careful to do it close to his clothes so blood can soak into them. I push on the knife. It's harder than it should be, but I am not too surprised. I don't push too deep, and I try the same thing on other parts of his body, with the same result.

The monster's skin is surprisingly strong and thick.

I put my knife away and grab its hand. Before I continue, I look behind me. Hadwin, Sophie, and Damon have looks on their faces that are hard to describe.

I also notice the bus driver pushing people toward the bus, away from us and the three dead goblins. I guess he saw me poking the goblin with a knife, as I also see disgust on his face.

To be honest, I am surprised as well. Never in my life did I think I would do something like this, but I am surprisingly calm and clear-minded.

"You don't have to be here," I say.

Damon curses, but all of them stay.

I try punching it a few times, and the response I'm getting is much more resistant than hitting a human body. I am also unable to break his ribs after repeatedly hitting his chest with my fist and full strength.

I continue examining the goblin.

Its nose is smaller than a human's, even if we leave out proportions. Maybe it doesn't have a good sense of smell? That would be good, as I am worried that they will sniff out their companions.

Its ears are also small, but what worries me are its big eyes. They are almost twice as big as mine. I just hope they don't see twice as good. During the night, it would be bad news.

The creature also has pretty long nails; they are sharp, and if everything else fails, they can be used as weapons.

The creature's teeth are also extremely sharp. I'd be concerned about the risk of infection from a potential bite.

I don't find any pockets in its clothes, so other than weapons, this goblin didn't carry anything.

I can't be sure if that's the norm for them or if they move around like this.

I tell the results of my examination to the others and stand up.

Where are its heart and other vital organs located? What makes it so strong? Can it use mana, and if so, how does it affect its physiology? Is it particularly vulnerable to fire? What are its weak points? And where is its skin thinnest?

Answering most of those questions would create quite a mess.

Maybe next time.

After stretching a little bit, I focus and put two stat points into constitution and one into mana.

At the moment, I'm not sure if changes in investing stat points show up instantly or gradually. I'm more inclined to the second option, so investing in them sooner sounds like a good idea.

My survivability is most important at the moment. I believe that constitution increases my endurance and vitality and affects my regeneration.

At the moment, I don't have access to food, so a stronger body sounds like a good idea.

I just hope it doesn't mean increased consumption of calories to keep me going.

I am sure it does. We can't have things too easy, can we?

I don't need much strength, as I can use weapons and attack weak points.

Unfortunately, I'm not in a situation where I can test my stat points, as I need to find water, food, shelter, and fight against these monsters.

One point in mana is a risk, and I justify it as something that potentially can make me stronger.

But I can't lie to myself. It's simple curiosity, and I am willing to risk a little bit to satisfy it.

Ever since I felt it for the first time, I keep trying to use it manually with no success so far.

I was only able to use [Focus] and mana during fights. It happened subconsciously. When we found the goblins, I was able to control it a little bit.

I can't wait to test it out a bit more, but unfortunately, I have other priorities at the moment.

"I have a place in mind where we can get rid of them," Hadwin says. "I noticed it when we were scouting. It's a deep hole near a few big rocks, probably caused by a landslide. We can just throw them down there. It should be around fifteen minutes there and back"—he then looks at the goblin—"maybe twenty."

Chapter 11
Quests

It makes Damon start grumbling, but he surprisingly stands up and says, "Let's make it quick."

He lifts up his goblin, and a surprised look appears on his face. It looks like he did invest his stats.

He should have leveled up, and Sophie as well. I am pretty sure he put it all into strength, so I decide to watch him carefully to compare his increased strength to my constitution.

My theory is that my increased constitution means I can use my peak strength for longer, and I will need shorter rest times to be back at my peak form. I also have a suspicion that I will heal faster and have tougher skin and stronger bones, just like the goblin.

Increased strength should increase the density and strength of muscles. But it also comes up with a potential problem.

What if you invest too much into strength, but you don't have a body strong enough to handle it? Once again,

I become annoyed for not knowing and not being able to test it out as much as I want.

I also put the goblin on my shoulder, making sure to have my right hand free and ready to throw the body on the ground. At worst, I can use the goblin as a shield against an attack. Sophie also picks up the goblin quite easily.

Hmm. I guess that means that stat increase manifests fairly quickly. Few minutes maybe?

Hadwin puts the gun into his right hand and the goblin's spear in his left and starts leading us into the forest.

As we enter, I don't feel as pressured as before, but I am still careful. The wind is now stronger, so we can hear the rustling of leaves and creaking branches as they bend in the wind. The sun seems to be right over us.

I still twitch every time I hear an unexpected noise.

As before, Hadwin walks first, me to his left and Damon to his right. Sophie follows behind us. I notice that she moved the goblin slightly lower, to cover more of her back.

At this point, I am sure that the results of my increased constitution are showing, as I don't feel myself getting tired from carrying the creature. The only thing I notice is my empty stomach.

Food. I need lots of food. I glance at the goblin, but I instantly decide that I am not that hungry. Yet.

When we finally throw the goblins into the hole, I notice Damon's ragged breathing. He seems better than before, but it's easy to see how tired he is.

I am now also one hundred percent sure that he didn't put much into constitution.

Sophie seems to be better than him, so I guess that she put at least something into it.

On our way back, we are even more careful than before, but we move much quicker. Not being able to see what's behind the trees makes us all nervous.

When we get back to the bus, I feel relieved, even though there isn't too big a difference in our safety.

As I move away from people, I take a peek at my stats.

[Name: Nathaniel Gwyn]
Difficulty: Hell
Floor: 1
Time left until forced return: 4y 364d 20h 52m 59s
Level: 2
Strength: 6
Dexterity: 8
Constitution: 8
Mana: 3
[Primary Class: Unavailable]
[Subclass: Unavailable]
Skills:
Focus - Level 3
Mana Manipulation - Level 1
[Skill Points: 0]
[Stat Points: 0]

I let Hadwin and the others take care of annoying stuff, and sit on the ground, leaning once again against the bus's tire.

The wind brushes my hair as I close my eyes and slowly inhale the fresh air. It's so different from the air in the city. There's a hard-to-describe smell to it, slightly sweet, but not too overpowering.

I like it. Warm rays of the sun on my hands touch my skin, and other than the passengers, I don't hear anything: no cars, no machines, no planes.

It's quiet, almost peaceful, yet I know how dangerous this place is.

Also, it's called the first floor, so does that mean that the sun, wind, and sky are fake? There are probably other floors above or below us, or is it just a place on a distant planet? Is it the whole planet? Simulation?

At the moment, I'm curious about what will be in the sky tonight, but at the same time, I feel a hint of fear. It's hard enough to fight against unknown creatures during the day, but at night, with reduced visibility? Sure, we can set up a campfire, but that would be like running around the place and screaming that we're here.

I let out a sigh. We're screwed, aren't we? I have a feeling that we were insanely lucky until now.

The wolf seemed to be starved or wounded and without its pack. We got ambushed by only three goblins, but even then, Hadwin almost died, and the other two got injured.

There will be more of them. I'm sure of it. Should I leave? I glance back at the bus and try to ignore the discussion inside.

There are pros and cons to staying, but I feel like the pros outweigh the cons. I need someone to keep watch when I'm sleeping. Hadwin has a gun, so that's something, and it looks like the guy knows how to move around the forest. If we're going to stay here for five years, he would be useful.

I don't know how to hunt or skin animals.

Hell, I wouldn't even know how to set up a campfire or cook.

Then there are also others. I can collect some data just from watching them—stat point distribution, skills, and classes if we get to it.

Footsteps catch my attention, and a student emerges from behind the bus—a nineteen-year-old girl, slim, blond, and taller than me.

She briefly glances my way but then directs her focus toward the forest, leaning against the bus. Retrieving a cigarette and lighter from her pocket, she lights it up.

With her eyes closed, she slowly inhales, savoring the smoke.

"Haa... It will be really bad when I run out of cigarettes." Her voice is quiet as she slowly smokes, enjoying every whiff. "Do you want one?"

I just shake my head and stay quiet.

"So you did stop smoking... So responsible."

I still don't react. Let's see what she wants; it's not like we were ever super friendly with each other.

The girl stops when she is halfway through her cigarette and extinguishes it against the bus. Then she carefully puts it back inside the pack and then her pocket.

One minute.

Two minutes.

Five.

She is leaning in silence while looking toward the forest.

"Do you also think that we are in deep shit, Nat?" she whispers, still looking away.

Isn't that obvious?

"It all looks so normal...trees, grass, sky..." She falls silent after glancing at the sky. "You know, before we ended up here, I had a fight with my mom," she said, her voice even quieter now. "I called her..." She pauses for a moment, and a self-deprecating chuckle echoes in the surrounding silence.

She then continues to talk, and I don't do anything but listen. I can do that much for her. I feel like I owe her at least that much.

She turns back to face me. "Do you think I'm an asshole?"

I don't get it. Isn't what she thinks more important than my opinion?

I shrug my shoulders, and there is a slight disappointment in her eyes. Then she chuckles.

"I should have expected such an answer from you. Anyway, Kevin found out something. Just say '*quest window*.'" Before she disappears back inside, she asks, "Nat, will you help me if you can?"

I look up from the ground, and our eyes meet.

Obviously, my life is a priority. But if it doesn't put me in danger...

My answer is just a short nod.

Before she disappears from my sight, I see a hint of relief on her face.

"Quest window," I say out loud.

[Floor Quest]
Stay alive for 30 days
Rewards:
Entrance to the second floor
Access to Community
1 skill point
5 stat points
[Side Quest]
Stay alive for 24 hours.
Rewards:
Gear of your choice

CHAPTER 12
MANA

Okay.

Fine.

I am not a person who tends to get angry easily, but even I have my limits. If I ever meet the asshole who designed this thing, I will fuck them up.

Well, let's not think too much about it. My mind is most likely being read even at the moment, so it's better if I make some plans after I come up with a way to counter it.

Now then, mana.

I lie on the ground and roll under the bus.

Let's try it here. I need to focus, and I don't want to get hit by a ranged attack from the forest. We are pretty far from it, but I wouldn't be surprised.

I close my eyes and try to use [Focus]. I have already used it a few times, so I know the feeling I should have.

It's hard to activate it at will, but after ten minutes, I'm finally able to do it. It isn't as deep a focus as I was able to gain during fights, but it should be enough.

As I try to keep it activated, I start remembering the feeling of what I think is mana flowing through my body and strengthening it.

I start with my hand. While slowly breathing in and out, my focus deepens. What is it even? What needs to be done to turn something into a skill?

I quickly shake my head to get rid of useless thoughts and focus a bit more.

Sounds slowly fade out, and I can hear my heart beating slowly. Then I feel a slight tingling in my hand. It starts with my fingers and continues up to my wrist.

It's the same feeling as before.

By force, I calm down my now-faster heartbeat. I focus on the feeling and try to understand it. It's hard to explain. More than relying on my mind, I let my body do it.

Maybe it's like when you catch something falling down from a table, and in the end, it's just your body that reacts by itself—just a simple reflex.

It's only after you reflexively catch the falling item and hold it in your hands that you realize what just happened.

So here I am, trying not to think about it too much. Somehow it feels cringy.

Allow your heart to guide you.

Sense it deep within your soul.

Do not think, just do.

Let the force...

Goddamn. I just can't think of another way, not at the moment.

I try it again. The feeling extends up to my shoulder, and I squeeze my fist. I can't be sure it isn't a placebo, but I feel that my right hand is stronger than my left.

I furrow my brow. I have a feeling that if I said it out loud, someone would laugh at me. The system better not

be recording my current thoughts or streaming them somewhere.

So where is the mana coming from?

Sure, I have a mana stat, but what does it mean? Did I get another organ that is producing mana?

Is it just flowing through my body, or is it stored somewhere and moving to the part of my body I want it to?

Let's try again, and this time, slower.

I once again enter the focus and let my body take care of the rest. I feel strength in my right hand, but I just don't know where it came from.

I cancel it.

Again.

...

Again.

...

Again.

...

After around twenty more tries, and when I start feeling lightheaded, I finally feel it. A thin thread of mana connecting my heart and hand.

Don't tell me. I try it again, and now I focus on my heart right from the start.

I barely feel it, but mana forms there and then slowly flows through my veins, reaching my hand. It's not using only one vein but multiple veins.

So that's how it is.

I spend another half hour trying to feel my mana, and when I hear Hadwin calling my name, I find a new notification.

> **You have acquired [Mana Perception - Level 0]**
> **[Mana Manipulation - Level 1 > Mana**
> **Manipulation - Level 2]**

I guess it's something.

Under Hadwin's amused gaze, I roll out from under the bus and stand up. Other than that, he doesn't react to it, which makes it even worse.

Asshole.

"Do you want to join us for another expedition? Damon and Sophie are coming as well, and I have one place I want to check out a bit more."

I nod and grab my stuff, following him.

"I noticed a spot where it appears to slope downward. If we're fortunate, it could be a valley, and there may be a stream in the vicinity."

We come near the other two already waiting for us. Both of them hold short spears in their hands, the ones goblins used.

I guess it's better than nothing.

"Of course, we have to be careful. If there is water, then there is a high chance we will end up running into more animals or...other creatures."

"Anyone else joining us?"

Damon's answer is a derogatory laugh.

"They are busy shitting their pants every time they hear some noise."

Well, it's not unexpected.

"A few kids wanted to join, but I turned them down," Hadwin adds in between Damon's trash-talk.

I ignore Damon's mumbling as he continues complaining. Will I get a skill from it? Damon's trash-talk resistance Level 1?

Hmm, maybe if I try hard enough?

While I am trying to acquire a new skill with Damon's help, Sophie is saying goodbye to her sister. It's easy to see how worried she is.

Somehow, I can't help feeling a tiny bit jealous.

CHAPTER 13
TRAP

Seemingly having fallen into a habit, I am once again on the left, Damon on the right, and Sophie in the back as we follow Hadwin.

After just a few minutes of us clumsily sneaking, we stop at Hadwin's gesture. He just points in front of us, slightly to the left.

I frown, not noticing anything.

Leaves around a stone's throw in front of us start rustling, and I hear Sophie screaming in warning as the enemy also appears from behind.

Green creatures surround us—growling and showing their teeth.

Two Level 2 warriors, two Level 3 warriors, and one Level 5 goblin shaman.

Not good. Actually, it's pretty bad.

Really bad.

I get ready to run away when it becomes even worse. A car-sized wolf appears from behind the goblin shaman.

> ## [Reanimated Wolf - Level 2]

He's big, brown, and bloodied, but the most eye-catching thing is the iron pipe sticking out of its blinded eye.

I enter the deepest [Focus] I ever have.

The world around me quiets, colors lose some of their vibrancy, and my mind filters out useless information.

My and the goblin shaman's eyes meet, and I swear he looks like he is laughing. The goblins don't seem to be surprised to meet us at all.

Someone screams.

We don't even get time to run as the reanimated wolf rushes at us. Hadwin makes the first move, and I can hear gunshots.

One.

Two.

Three.

All of them hit, but the wolf keeps charging and only slightly staggers after every gunshot. There is no blood.

Its target is Hadwin, who quickly swaps to the spear.

As the wolf shortens the distance, I put my knife away and hold my pipe in both hands. I let mana flow through my body, focusing more of it on my shoulders and waist as I burrow my feet into the ground.

I clench my core, twist at my waist, and swing with all the strength I can muster.

The wolf passes by me, aiming for Hadwin. I hit its front leg.

Something cracks really loudly, and the weapon in my hands bends. The wolf staggers, but there is no painful cry as it falls down while stepping on its broken leg. Hadwin quickly stabs with his spear.

But I am already behind the three and making a circle to the left toward the other goblins, knife back in my left hand. Mana is still flowing through my body.

I would like to save some and turn the skill off when I don't need it, but I want to stay as careful as I can.

The goblin shaman is holding his hands in the air and mumbling something under his breath, his eyes glued to me. One Level 3 stays near him, and another Level 3 slowly walks toward me together with a Level 2. The last goblin is already fighting with Damon while Sophie is helping Hadwin with the wolf.

The Level 2 goblin stabs at me with his spear; his moves are painfully amateurish. With my body strengthened by mana, I easily dodge it and hit his face in exchange, breaking his nose and injuring an eye.

As he steps back with a painful groan, I move to the left and kick the dashing Level 3 goblin. My leg hurts from it, but as he staggers, I dash back into his reach while he is regaining balance.

I stab my dagger as deep as I can into his neck and twist, breaking it in the process.

He falls to the ground, twitching his limbs, letting out wet, choking noises.

Good.

After dodging one more attack, I finish off the Level 2 goblin with multiple hits on his head from my iron pipe. His skull cracks, and he falls down without much resistance.

The whole time, I kept a few trees between me and the goblin shaman. The fight took less than ten seconds.

Before continuing, I pick up both of their spears and peek at the duo. The shaman seems to be done with whatever he was doing, and now he is only waiting.

I peek just for a second and throw a spear at him. The weapon is terribly balanced, and it just hits the ground a few meters away from him.

It's harder than I thought.

When I glance backward, I see that Damon's Level 2 goblin is already dead, and they seem to be finishing off the wolf. Hadwin is limping with a deep wound in his thigh, and Sophie's hand seems to be wounded, too. Damon is pressing a wound on his chest.

I have an opportunity, but something stops me from running away, and I turn back to the duo in front of me.

I bend to pick a few stones from the ground when I hear it. A terrible, piercing noise.

Not good.

Without even thinking, I dash to the side as quickly as I can.

Boom.

Something explodes, and I feel a pressure wave hitting my back, throwing me against a tree.

Even before the pain hits me, I know I have broken a few bones, but I try to roll as soon as I hit the ground.

I limp a few meters, then *boom.*

Another shockwave throws me to the ground. The world around me starts spinning, and I taste blood.

NOT GOOD.

I let mana flow through my body and crawl back on my legs. They are not broken, but one of my arms is and uselessly hangs at my side. That leaves my iron pipe on the ground unavailable. The spear I picked up is broken, and I am just holding its upper half.

As expected, the Level 3 goblin is already next to me, and this time, I am unable to fully dodge his swift stab.

The spear grazes my side, and the goblin grabs my broken arm, sending a painful impulse through me and making me scream in pain.

But I stay focused. I keep mana flowing through my body. Even battered like this, I feel confident.

He will die.

My heart is beating like crazy, pumping mana and blood through my veins.

My breathing is ragged but steady.

It hurts so much. But even in such a state, there is not a single speck of doubt in my mind.

I will win.

Then I kick the goblin between his legs.

He lets out a painful groan and bends slightly. I swing a broken spear and stab into the goblin's neck.

My spear doesn't enter too deeply. So, with a loud scream, I pull back, thrust again, and give him another kick between his legs.

He lets out a suffocating noise as blood starts flowing from his neck and mouth. He bends more while trying to cover his lower parts. As he does so, I strike his chin with my knee.

Even in such a state, my kick is powerful enough, and I see consciousness disappear from his eyes.

As he falls down, I fall on him and stab his neck a few more times. In the back of my mind, I hear a notification.

While holding a bloodied, broken spear in my hand, I stand up.

One more.

CHAPTER 14
SHAMAN

It's painful. It's tiring. But I get up and squeeze the bloodied half-spear in my right hand. The rusty smell of blood hits my nose. My other arm is uselessly hanging alongside my body, broken somewhere under my shoulder. I can't even move it without pain making my vision spin.

The goblin shaman is standing there mumbling with one of his hands pointing toward me.

I let go of the broken spear and grab a stone from the ground, instantly throwing it at the goblin.

Surprisingly, his chanting pauses, and he frowns. Instead of hitting him, the stone slows on the approach and falls about a meter away from him.

I do it again and get the same result.

His mumbling stops, and the stone drops around three meters away from him. He screams something, and I quickly jump behind a tree, but there is no terrible noise, and the tree doesn't explode. Instead, I can hear him chanting once again.

Then I hear a gunshot.

All of us freeze for a second, and unnatural silence fills the surroundings.

Another gunshot.

Hadwin is pointing his gun at the shaman. Surprisingly, the green creature isn't dead. Not even wounded. The same thing happens to the bullet as to stones.

As it enters an area close to the goblin, it slowly travels through the air before it lands next to him.

"Damn..." Hadwin's voice is tired, and he is slowly limping.

Yet he seems to be in the best state out of the three of us. Sophie is holding a piece of cloth on her wounded hand while glaring at the goblin shaman. Damon is sitting on the ground and leaning against a tree. I'm not sure if he is conscious or even alive.

The goblin looks at us, his gaze full of hate. He bares his sharp teeth, and a deep, hissy growl escapes from his mouth.

I move my tired body toward him, and the only thing I can think about is killing him.

I throw a few things at him as I walk closer, a stone, a branch, a piece of hardened dirt. Every time, they just slow in the air and fall down near him. But every time I do it, his chant pauses, and his face becomes angrier and angrier.

"You don't like that, do you?" I smirk, and I can taste the blood in my mouth.

I spit it out while continuing to walk closer and throwing stuff at him.

"You green piece of shit."

He keeps letting out terrible noises, maybe even words. He doesn't seem worried at all as I stop just a few meters away from him.

Is that a smile on his face?

Fucker.

I stab at him, but at some distance away from him, it starts feeling weird, as if the spear is moving through molasses, and the feeling becomes worse the closer it gets to the goblin.

After around one meter, my stab loses all its strength.

When I try to quickly pull it back, it becomes even worse, as if it's stuck in something.

So I just let go of the spear, and it slowly falls down to the ground, almost like a feather.

The goblin's grin becomes even wider, and he chants faster.

You are so dead.

I step toward the goblin, and for a moment, his smile becomes even wider. Then it instantly disappears from his face, replaced by sheer shock.

I enter the zone around him while moving really slowly. I am not attacking him at all, just taking a step toward him. A really slow step.

There is some resistance, almost like moving underwater, and when I try quickly moving with just my finger, the resistance becomes much stronger.

So that's how it is.

Amazing.

His smile disappears, and it seems like he did stutter for a moment before resuming his chanting.

I continue slowly moving toward him. My body is turned slightly with my wounded arm facing him.

After entering the zone, an arm's reach away from him, I feel the resistance weaken slightly.

The goblin finally gives up his chanting, and a dagger appears in his hand. He is moving slowly, also affected by the field around him.

I focus once again and try to send the last drops of mana through my body.

The shaman seems to be an even worse fighter than the other goblins, as he just stabs at my chest.

I am already dodging even before he makes a stabbing motion.

His feet's placement.

His stance.

The way he turns his body.

I predict where he is going to stab and move my body slightly to make him barely miss me.

When his dagger enters my reach, I notice fear in his eyes. He slowly realizes that he is going to miss, and I can see his body struggle. Muscles twitching, his expression turning darker and darker.

Why did you stop smiling? Is it not fun anymore?

Smile for me.

He tries to move as much as he can and change the direction of his stab. Then he tries to quickly pull his attack back, panic in his movements.

But he can't. He is also restricted by the unnatural field around his body.

As he starts pulling back his dagger for another stab, I grab his throat. I focus most of my remaining mana into my hand and try to bury the tips of my fingers into the front of his neck.

The monster attempts to escape, but I follow him at the same speed, and he keeps panicking more and more.

He keeps trying to move faster than he can and keeps getting restricted. Meanwhile, I just slowly follow his movement at the speed the field allows me to.

There is another stab coming. From the way he moves, I know that if I dodge it, he will continue and try to stab the hand holding his neck.

I should dodge.

It's smart to dodge.

But I just shift my body, and his dagger enters my broken hand instead.

The pain is terrible, much worse than I expected. The dagger is slowly penetrating my skin, tearing my muscles, and scratching my bone.

But I don't let go. Instead, I squeeze his neck harder and harder. He is already scratching my right hand with his remaining hand, leaving deep, bloody grooves on my forearm.

I am almost worried that I will break my teeth from clenching them so hard. It's easily the most pain I've ever felt in my life.

He then twists the dagger in my hand, and I feel tears running down my cheeks.

I can't help it, but a painful groan escapes from my mouth. But I don't let go.

I squeeze harder and harder.

I feel the blood from his neck on my fingers, and then I finally penetrate the softer skin of his neck. It feels disgusting.

Blood flows down his neck and on my hands as I grab his Adam's apple and start pulling it out of his neck. In the process, I lose the last drops of my mana.

Then I hear soft noise as if something is breaking—his necklace falls apart.

The feeling of my body being deep underwater instantly disappears.

The goblin shaman falls down on the ground while putting his hands against the hole in his neck. Blood flows through his fingers, and he lets out noises I already want to forget about.

After a few seconds of struggling, the light disappears from his eyes.

Only a terrible, hateful expression stays on his face until the last moment he stares at me.

CHAPTER 15
WE SHOULD TALK

[You have defeated a Goblin - Level 3]
[You have defeated a Goblin - Level 2]
[You have defeated a Goblin - Level 3]
[You have defeated a Reanimated Wolf - Level 2]
[You have defeated a Goblin Shaman - Level 5]
[Level 2 > Level 3]

I instantly put two points into constitution and one into mana. My body feels terrible. Every muscle feels as if it's about to tear. I feel weak.

I'm also so terribly hungry.

"Are you fine? Do you need..."

Just leave me alone.

"Nathaniel." The voice becomes louder.

Screw off.

I slowly calm down by breathing.

Calm down. Focus on breathing in and out. Filter out the pain. A little bit is fine.

Good.

Now put more strength into your legs.

Good.

Now fall down and scratch your knees and palms, adding to your wounds.

Goo... What?

...

Damn.

I clench my teeth—deep breath.

Yes, like this.

A bit more strength into the left leg.

Good.

More strength in the right leg.

Nice.

Now turn to Hadwin and try to look a bit more friendly and not like someone who tore off the neck of a living being. Do it slowly so that your head won't spin.

When I turn around, I see a worried look on his face. I notice the fact that he's still holding a gun in his hand. I'm sure that it's just a coincidence that he's pointing it slightly in my direction.

Just in case, I try to predict the way he would lift it up if he wanted to shoot. I slightly shift my body.

If he moves that way, I can rush him. Forget about using my hands; I will hit his nose with my forehead.

He might be able to shoot me, but before he does so, I can slightly move his hand so it won't kill me.

Probably.

"Goddamn, Nat. You look terrible."

No shit, asshole.

I nod slowly.

Hadwin puts his weapon away, and I feel the tension in my body dissipate. Instead, I focus on our surroundings.

"Let's keep our guard up. And I need a weapon," I mutter.

I lower my body slightly, and another wave of pain attacks me as I grab the shaman's dagger and wipe the blood on my fingers onto my once-white shirt.

I also grab pieces of his broken necklace and put them into my pocket.

"We have to go quickly. Sophie and Damon are also wounded, but they should be okay. Thankfully, they leveled up and put all their points into constitution. That should help them a little bit," Hadwin says, looking at me. "How are you?"

"I'm fine. Let's move."

The points I invested seem to be doing their part. Just a little bit, but it's not like I can complain. Of course, I still feel terrible. The hunger I'm feeling is like there's a big empty hole in my stomach, and I bet that soon enough, my stomach will start digesting itself.

As I'm walking, I let some mana flow through my body. It's not a big difference, but it's slowly becoming easier and easier. A small, really small, but noticeable difference.

Damon is still unconscious, and Sophie is breathing weakly while holding her terribly wounded hand. I'm surprised she hasn't passed out.

"Nat," Hadwin says.

"Take Damon. I will follow with Sophie in a minute."

"...Be careful on your way back."

He puts Damon over one of his shoulders while holding the gun in his free hand and disappears between the trees.

Huh, he agreed pretty easily.

After a few seconds, I start counting.

One minute.

Two.

Sophie starts nervously looking at me.

Three.

"We should—" she begins but stops when I lift up my finger.

"We should talk."

"There is no time. We don't even know if there are more of them..." She moves closer to me, trying to hide, but I can see that she's getting nervous. "We can talk when we get back."

Does she still think this is Earth? I put my hand on her wounded hand and squeeze.

A painful scream escapes her mouth, and I feel a slight urge to let go, but at this point, I don't even know if these are my feelings.

"W-what are you doing?" she screams while attempting to move away from me, but I hold her and squeeze harder.

She screams again but quickly quiets down while looking around with teary eyes.

Looking for help? Scared that there will be more monsters? I am also worried about that, but right now, there is something much more important.

My mind is only mine.

Her face scrunches up, and I realize I've been squeezing even harder.

Am I really that angry? Hmm. Let's think about it logically since I can't trust my feelings at the moment.

I think what she did is something that would make me angry. Really angry.

My freedom is one of the most important things to me ever since I was young.

To be honest, I am surprised I am not angrier.

Is she influencing me even now?

Her chest moves up and down as she keeps her wet green eyes on me, almost pleading.

In the end, she's just a young woman.

"Let's talk later. Please?"

Her voice is shaking, and there is a drop of blood on her bottom lip from how hard she is biting it.

"Let's just go..."

"Did you... Are you using a skill on me?"

"We need to go."

For a moment, I don't say anything.

She avoids my gaze, and I can feel her muscles tensing. Her mouth opens slightly, but no sound escapes her.

Shock? Guilt?

I stay quiet.

"I don't know... I don't know what you mean."

A scream of pain, more tears in her eyes.

"You need to calm down and listen to me..." She puts her free hand on my shoulder, pleading. "We really need to go. It's not safe here."

My anger weakens even more. Is her skill stronger with skin contact?

"We can talk when we get back. Nathaniel?"

My feelings are one big mess.

"One more chance, Sophie. No more lies, okay?"

She tries to open her mouth, but I gesture for her to stop.

"Think about your sister before you say something."

Then it hits me. Terrible, terrible fear I have never felt in my life.

I barely stop myself from shaking, and I feel cold sweat running down my back. I almost want to scream, let go of everything, and just run away.

My heartbeat speeds up, and my limbs become cold.

Chapter 16
Death

So terrifying. So amazing.

I am clenching my teeth so hard that they feel like they are about to break. Goose bumps are all over my body.

I am cold and shaking.

It's hard to even think, and [Focus] is the only thing stopping me from running away.

Really amazing.

How does it work? How did she get the skill? Is she using mana? How many emotions can she manipulate? How many people can she affect at once? Is it a Level 1 skill? If yes, how strong can it get? And probably the most important question is can I use her to survive? Can she use it on monsters?

Did she use it only on me during the fight or on the goblins as well?

Did she use it on the goblins to make them attack me instead of Hadwin and Damon, leaving three of them to deal only with the wolf and one goblin?

Maybe?

"Interesting..." I whisper, and I mean it. The feelings I'm experiencing at the moment feel so real. It's not hard to imagine how dangerous she will be if she gets time to develop her skills.

She could slowly manipulate someone instead of using raw power like she is now, and her target wouldn't even have to realize it.

"DO. NOT. DARE," she hisses through her teeth.

How scary.

"I will fucking kill you if you dare to touch her!"

"Good," I say. "Think about it this way. For me, my mind is the same as your sister is for you."

"I...will kill you..."

I interrupt her. "I think we may have started on the wrong foot." I let her lean onto me, and we start walking toward our camp. I try to ignore the agonizing pain from my wounded arm and almost have to pull her as she resists.

Let's risk it.

Sure, I almost died because of her, but I am alive. In the future, her skill can become amazingly useful. Hell, it's super useful even now.

I pause, and terrifying thoughts flash through my mind. Is she manipulating me now? Did I switch from killing her to using her because of her mind manipulation?

I know I am playing with fire, but I think I can now recognize when she is trying to manipulate my feelings, and her usefulness can outweigh all the risks.

Obviously, in a perfect world, I wouldn't have to be worried about all of that.

Now I will have to become stronger faster than she is. That way, she won't be able to control me.

I believe I can do it. I trust in my decisions and my skill. I trust in myself.

So let's keep her around. I won't get rid of a weapon I can use to keep myself alive, and if she does try something and I survive, well, that will be the end for her sister. The thought of hurting an innocent kid disgusts me, but if I have to pick between me and her life, I won't hesitate.

If Sophie and I fight, I will either go after her sister or the little girl won't be able to survive without Sophie in case she dies.

Who else would care about a little girl they don't know when fighting for their life?

Sophie isn't dumb.

"So let's start over again, yes?"

But I won't forget. I will always remember that she tried to use me as a shield and pushed me into fights without even caring about my life. I don't care that she was scared or that she tried to take care of her sister.

I let a small smile appear on my face.

"Let's be allies, Sophie."

I won't forget.

We stay quiet for the rest of the way back.

Thankfully, we don't meet anyone while moving back to the bus. Our way back takes even longer than before because we're wounded.

My wound isn't bleeding anymore but feels like it is burning, and my arm is still useless. The effect of an

increased constitution is noticeable, but there are questions as well.

Do I require more calories now? Five thousand? Ten thousand? Are there animals and monsters that can give me more calories, or will I need to eat all the time? Will there be a point where I can't get enough food or won't need to eat at all?

Do I even need to sleep? Well, I feel tired, so probably yes, but what if I invest more points into constitution?

Another thing is that all my smaller wounds, such as scratches, are either fully healed or close to it. It's not like I can see the wounds closing right in front of my eyes, but they are healing quite quickly.

Hadwin quickly joins us as soon as we leave the forest, and I leave Sophie to the boy who is following him.

"I was starting to worry. It took you a long time."

Sophie just glances at me but stays quiet, and I shrug my shoulders.

As we get closer to the middle of the clearing, I notice Damon lying on the ground.

Unmoving. Pale.

"He didn't make it..." says Hadwin quietly.

His eyes are closed and his face is empty, maybe slightly sad. It's really hard to read.

Did he...? Damon didn't look like he was about to die the last time I saw him. The clothes around his chest are terribly bloodied, and his expression is anything but peaceful.

Sophie seems to be fairly shocked. "We talked just a few minutes ago... How could it..." She trails off.

There were no last words. No meaningful fight. Just one goblin barely reaching his chest and one undead wolf.

In a fight where three of them fought against two opponents, Damon still died.

The wolf moved even slower than the first time we met him, the goblin was only Level 2, and they were armed. Hadwin even had a gun, and yet...he still died.

Just like that.

How? How are they that weak? Should I bother staying with them?

"Nat..."

I might be better on my own.

"Nat."

I am stronger than all of them.

"Nathaniel."

Should I even waste my time by helping them to develop? It might be better to invest all of that time into myself.

Someone touches my shoulder, and I feel as if I woke up.

What happened? I notice my palm bleeding from my fingernails digging into it.

Oh.

Seems like Sophie isn't the only one shaken.

I glance at the blond girl holding my shoulder. She is and always was taller than me, even though she is younger. Her steel-gray eyes are calm, and for a moment, we just look at each other.

She smells of cigarettes.

Focus on breathing. I let out a little bit of mana and feel myself entering [Focus]—just a little bit.

One heartbeat.

My heart pushes mana through my veins. It is flowing in the same pathway as my blood, just slightly faster.

Two heartbeats.

All unused mana is circulating back to my heart and then is sent back to my body.

Three.

Tension slowly escapes my body.

Four.

Slow and deep breath in. Yes, good.

Five.

I exit [Focus], and I feel as if the haze covering my mind and eyes disappears.

"Can you hear me now?"

I nod.

"Good, let me help you with your wound."

She pulls me toward the bus, and I follow her without words.

CHAPTER 17
SKILLS

She is quiet the entire time. No questions, no bothering me. She just slowly cleans my wound as best as she can without water and with just a small piece of cloth.

She always knew me too well. I guess that's why I always felt comfortable around her.

The wound looks terrible even after some healing, thanks to my constitution.

While she does her stuff, I drink the last few drops of water remaining in my bottle. I store the empty bottle inside my bag.

"I don't know what else I should do. Pour alcohol over it? I don't have any. Burn it? I've only seen that in movies, so it might not work. And someone already took the first aid kit from the bus."

Her face remains calm throughout, and I notice she put her long hair into a pigtail, resting on her back. She is also not wearing her skirt anymore and is wearing leggings instead.

I look up from the ground. She is looking at me with an expectant expression on her face. I pause.

Why is it so easy to understand her?

"You can come with me next time I go into the forest."

I don't have to say more.

Slow nod.

> **[Name: Nathaniel Gwyn]**
> **Difficulty:** Hell
> **Floor:** 1
> **Time left until forced return:** 4y 364d 20h 9m 59s
>
> **Level:** 3
> **Strength:** 6
> **Dexterity:** 8
> **Constitution:** 10
> **Mana:** 4
>
> **[Primary Class: Unavailable]**
> **[Subclass: Unavailable]**
> **Skills:**
> Focus – Level 3
> Mana Manipulation – Level 2
> Mana Perception – Level 1
> **[Skill Points: 0]**
> **[Stat Points: 0]**

What the hell? Not even four hours? Is it bugged? It has to be, right? There is no way that we have only been here for four hours. It feels much longer.

"Tess," I say, speaking her name for the first time since we arrived here. She is my...old friend. Things between us are quite complicated.

"Yes?"

"I'm hungry."

Tess doesn't answer that.

Well, I tried.

"How is your wound?" she asks instead.

I move my hand slightly. It hurts, so I stop quickly. I will have to rely on my constitution to heal it, but for now, my hand isn't usable. The wound on my side also hurts every time I try to turn around.

Drops of sweat are forming on my forehead, and I feel hot.

"Arm's unusable," I say.

"I thought as much."

She pokes my left hand slightly, and a smile flickers in her eyes when I furrow my brow.

Her face stays the same, without expression.

"What are your stats?"

There is a short pause, but she doesn't think about it for too long and quickly tells me.

It's something like this.

> **Level:** 0
> **Strength:** 4
> **Dexterity:** 7
> **Constitution:** 2
> **Mana:** 1

Her stats are a bit lower than my starting ones, but they aren't bad at all. I also know she can fight a little bit, which is more than I can say about others.

"When you level up, put two points into constitution and one into mana. You can do it even without talking. Just think hard about putting your points into the stats you want."

Then I continue to tell her about the goblins we met, the goblin shaman, and the animated wolf.

I try to tell her anything she can find useful. The way they usually attack, the weapons I saw them use, and everything I know so far about mana.

Tess also got two skills.

> **[Psychokinesis]**
> **[Farsight]**

She told me that there are passengers with skills such as [Reflection], [Absorption], [Telekinesis], [Detection], and [Strengthening]. There is even one person with my [Focus] and another one with her [Psychokinesis].

To be honest, I did expect each skill to be unique to a person, so this surprises me a little bit.

Some people even started with three points in mana. Weird.

Mana is usually a resource used to cast magic, enchant items, create spells, and is used as some sort of fuel for magic items.

And it fascinates me. A lot. If I could, I would most likely spend hours just experimenting with it. It just feels like I'm a kid once again, and I got something amazing to play with. Something very few have. Mysterious and so full of opportunities.

Unfortunately, I have no such luxury.

Tess is almost done smoking a cigarette when Hadwin appears. He is followed by two men who both seem to be around thirty to forty years old. I noticed them before, and they seem to be fairly close to each other, probably two friends or coworkers.

Still limping, Hadwin opens his mouth and closes it after taking a look at my wound. I can see that he is fighting inside, and in the end, he decides to be shameless.

"Nat, I will need you." He shrugs and moves awkwardly.

At least he knows how shameless he is. But it's not like I can blame him. I'm sure I'm more useful than most people, even in the state I'm in. And it's not like I didn't expect him to come.

"When I was walking back with Damon..." He pauses for a second and continues after taking a deep breath. "I saw the river down the valley. Probably five minutes of walking away from the place where we met them..."

At the moment, I am not sure if it's all just an act or if he really feels bad for asking me.

How many bullets does he have left? It can't be many. One magazine? Two? Or is he already at the last one?

"Cassian and Dominic are going to join us."

Cassian is a shorter man with black hair, while Dominic has dark skin and curly hair. Both of them are in good shape, having figures that come from doing hard manual work.

I find it weird that they would want to join, even after seeing Damon's dead body. I think it's better to go, but people rarely use logic in such situations. Maybe...

I look at Sophie, who is standing nearby with her sister. Whatever.

I slowly stand up and try to calculate Cassian and Dominic's reach by looking at their arm lengths, and I assess their mobility by observing the way they move.

Let's see how you'll do.

"I'll be taking Tess with us, but I'll need a bit longer to rest. One hour should be okay. Oh, and give her one of the spears."

As I enter the bus, I hear Cassian and Dominic complaining.

I can't trust anyone. Not Sophie, not Hadwin. So I have to push, forget about my wounds, and get the last bit of energy from my body.

Because I am sure I will be in danger the moment they become stronger than I am.

CHAPTER 18
FASCINATION

Right after I reach the back seat, I take out my phone. Even before it turns on, I put the earbuds into my ears and turn on noise-canceling. The world instantly quiets down.

I connect the earbuds to the phone and scroll down through my playlist. Randomly, I pick one song and set it to play on repeat.

When I close my eyes, everything disappears. The voices of people around me, the lady sitting a few seats in front of me with her dog, a bunch of students, and twins.

I let it play two times before I start feeling better and let myself think a little bit.

I'm a wreck. My hand hurts more than I'm letting them know. I feel weak, lightheaded, and my muscles hurt, most likely from using mana.

I am thirsty and hungry.

My clothes are dirty. My shirt is more red and black than white at this point.

I glance at my phone. It's at seventy-eight percent. Earbuds are at seventy percent, and the case should have one more charge left.

I keep digging the nails of my fingers into my palm, and the wound keeps healing a little bit every time I do so.

My arm heals much slower, but there is some progress. I increase the volume and close my eyes again.

[Focus].

The song keeps playing in the background as I try to manipulate my mana and send it toward my wound. I keep imagining the wound closing. I am trying to "feel" it.

While I do so, I keep wounding my palm.

Obviously, it doesn't work, but it calms me down as I focus on the mana flowing through my body.

It feels weird, as if I got a new sense that's just for feeling the mana.

There are some losses as I circulate mana through my veins, in and out of my heart. But, at this point, I can't even feel where little bits of mana disappear. I don't even feel how mana comes into existence. I just know it starts at the heart.

But why does it travel through blood?

Is it just using my veins as a road through my body, or does it need to be mixed with blood?

Is my heart some kind of generator creating mana, or is it getting it from somewhere else and sending it through my body?

At this point, I don't even hear the music and don't realize that I am draining my phone's and earbuds' batteries.

Fascinated by mana, I keep feeling it as it travels through my body. Sometimes I slightly poke it.

How is it possible that I can manipulate it?

Is it because it's inside my body? Because it's my mana? Can I manipulate it even outside of my body?

Can I manipulate the mana of other people?

Time loses its meaning, and I hear notifications, but I ignore them. Amazed, I just keep moving mana inside my body. It's somehow calming.

What will I be able to do with it in the future? Where are the limits?

I move the mana to the tip of my finger. It reaches the furthest capillary, and then I push it out. It travels through the meat of my finger and skin. It feels like I am spending it faster and using more of it than when it goes through my veins. I push a little bit more of it, and it exits through my finger. It doesn't hurt me, and the consistency is like smoke, so I add more and more.

My head hurts.

Knock, knock.

Slow breath in.

Breathe out.

[Focus].

I push more, and I feel as if the mana is reaching a centimeter away from my finger. I focus on it. Make it thinner and sharper.

I feel like I don't have enough air, my brain hurting as I hear ringing in my ears.

More.

Notification.

KNOCK, KNOCK.

More.

I focus.

More mana, sharper, stronger. Use it, shape it, and add density. Much more density.

With a swipe, I move my finger across the side panel of the bus.

More pain and the mana disappears from the tip of my finger.

My hand starts shaking, and my finger hurts as if it got stuck in a closing door.

But it's there.

A deep graze in the side panel of the bus.

When I finally turn to the side and look at Cassian knocking on the window, I feel much better, even though my head is hurting.

POV – TESS HANSEN

Nathaniel disappears inside the bus as Cassian and Dominic start complaining. Hadwin quickly calms them down. Then, without any hesitation, Hadwin gives me one of the spears they were able to acquire. I also notice that he is far less pleasant and patient while dealing with the duo than with Nathaniel. His voice is much more commanding and firm.

The two men leave, not forgetting to give me a few nasty looks as they go. Hadwin gives me a short look and then also leaves. He doesn't even bother talking to me. His eyes just scan me up and down while checking how I hold the spear before he leaves.

I watch him as he slowly strips dead Damon of his clothes and shoes and then pulls his body close to the edge of the forest. The pale body of a tall, muscular man just lies

there in his underwear. There is a lot of loose skin over his body, like he's lost a lot of weight.

So that's it for you, Damon Beck. I didn't know him that well, and I am sure Nathaniel didn't even recognize him, as he looked so different after losing so much weight.

But I know for sure that Damon recognized Nathaniel. How could he not? You can't forget such a beating.

He once visited the gym Nathaniel liked to use and got beaten to a pulp after attacking him. I didn't see it, but from what I heard, he got both of his hands broken, and since then, he hated the younger boy.

Surprisingly, one more memory flashed to my mind: that of a younger Damon smiling brightly while lifting up his little sister, both of them laughing at some stupid joke.

The memory disappears, and there is only a dead body.

I sigh, then I hold my spear tighter and start practicing stabbing movements. I do it for half an hour to get used to the spear and the movement. Then I try to use my skills by following Nathaniel's guidance. Even though he said it feels awkward, I try to let my body handle it instead of trying to imagine it in my head.

At one point, a stone in the palm of my hand jumps slightly, but that's it.

An hour passes, and Cassian comes closer and knocks on the window. He knocks louder and louder until the young man inside finally starts moving toward the exit.

"...Prick," I hear Cassian say under his breath.

Nathaniel finally exits the bus. He is twenty-one years old, with black hair and a face that could be called handsome if it weren't for his permanently expressionless look. Because of that, he just appears unapproachable and unfriendly, and people rarely bother to talk to him.

The most striking part of him is his eyes. One eye is a deep, rich brown, while the other is soft gray. Heterochromia.

He stops in front of Cassian. Nathaniel is slightly taller, and his figure is slimmer. The man looks much more muscular. Yet he doesn't say anything, and after a bit, he just avoids his gaze, and Nathaniel passes by him. I notice that Cassian is clenching his hands as he does so.

"Any results?" Nathaniel asks as he stops in front of me. His eyes briefly scan my face, then he looks into my eyes for a split second and averts his gaze.

He keeps shifting his gaze—to the weapon in my hand, to my shoulders, to the side of the bus, to the forest in the distance. His eyes sweep over the surroundings with an unusual calm, as if absorbing every detail.

I share the results of my training without trying to exaggerate or lie, and he simply nods in response. Surprisingly, he looks back into my eyes again, for a second time in a few minutes. That's unusual for him. It seems like something made him happy, but I don't even bother asking him about it. I know he wouldn't like it.

At the moment, he's the only one I can rely on, so I have to stay on his good side and follow his orders. He's fair, so in exchange, he'll help me, too.

I don't have many options. It's either this or...

My eyes stop at the body at the edge of the clearing.

Chapter 19
Eyes Glowing Like Embers

Cassian is already with Hadwin and Dominic when I reach them. Only Hadwin greets me, while the other two mostly ignore me.

I also notice Damon's body at the edge of the clearing. He is only in his underwear, a massive wound on his chest.

I guess there is at least someone thinking a little bit. Even clothes can be useful, and it's not like we can go and buy some. What I don't like is that they didn't even bother to pull him a few meters further, in between trees.

Anyway, not my problem.

"What do we have for water?" I ask.

"A few bottles, a few plastic bags, and we also found this pretty big canister." He points at the iron canister near his legs. It's pretty big, probably for spare fuel or some other liquid.

I am not washing it, for sure. Sounds like a job for our newbies!

I just nod while pulling a knife from behind my waistband to hold it in my unwounded hand. It feels nice and heavy, much better than the knife I broke. Yet it's still made from some kind of stone, crystal, or something.

I would much prefer a spear so I can keep some distance from enemies we might meet, but it would be pretty difficult to use one with only one hand.

And I think I prefer a sharp blade over a blunt iron pipe. Sure, the reach is shorter, but if I aim right, I can do more damage.

"Let's go, then," Hadwin says and starts leading us toward the forest.

As we enter, I glance back and notice Sophie staring at me while holding her sister's hand. Her face is hard to read.

Tess, Cassian, and Dominic become really quiet as we start walking under the trees. They twitch every time we hear some noise, unsurprisingly. They saw us coming back wounded multiple times already, and someone even died, so it's not much of a surprise.

But this time, there is no attack, not even as we start walking down the hill near the place Hadwin talked about.

I like it.

I really do.

Let's keep it up.

Everyone perks up when we hear the sound of flowing water after a few more minutes. Cassian and Dominic instantly start excitedly whispering something, and even Hadwin speeds up his tempo.

After a few more meters, we exit the tree line and see a small stream of water flowing through the forest.

"Finally, we found it!" Cassian screams and rushes ahead of Hadwin.

"Shut up, Cassian!" Hadwin hisses and grabs his hand, pulling him back. "Remember where we are!"

Unfortunately, Cassian doesn't seem to be taking it seriously. He smirks and nods, nearly ignoring Hadwin, unaware of the danger he might put us in. So I calmly put away the knife I hold.

"Hey." I keep my voice soft, almost whispering, and when he turns to me, I bury my knee into his belly.

Air escapes his mouth, and there is no cry because of that. Eyes wide open. Face grimacing from the pain. Before he gets back to his senses, I squeeze his neck.

In the corner of my vision, I notice Dominic wanting to charge at me, but Tess steps into his way and points the spear at him.

Silence.

No movement.

"Stay quiet, okay?"

Cassian hesitates for a bit and then opens his mouth to say something, so I squeeze harder. After a few more seconds, he realizes it and just quickly nods.

He gasps for breath when I let go of his neck, and I grab my dagger from the ground.

If he wants to die, sure, go ahead, but I won't let him risk my life by acting stupid.

I nod to Hadwin, and he nods back. While I am keeping watch, he moves closer to the water. From where I am, it seems fairly normal, and hopefully, it's safe to drink.

Hmmm. Just to be sure, let's have others drink it first after we boil it. If they are fine after a few hours, I can drink it, too.

Ah, the good ol' "human guinea pig" approach, always a classic. Finally, they are going to do something useful.

Hadwin and the two men quickly start filling the canister, bottles, and a few plastic bags with water, while Tess and I keep watch.

When they are almost done, Tess gestures at me and puts a finger to her lips while pointing somewhere between the trees. That makes me squeeze the weapon in my hand.

"Movement," I warn the others, and all three of them let go of the stuff in their hands and grab their weapons. I hear a click from Hadwin's handgun.

Tess points at herself and then toward the source of movement.

She seems determined as she looks at me, most likely waiting for my approval.

Well, she seems fairly confident, so I just nod.

Both of us go between the trees while I gesture for the others to stay. After a few seconds of walking, Tess stops. She grabs her spear as if she is about to throw it, and then she does just that.

The spear flies out of her hand surprisingly quickly, and I would swear it changed its trajectory a little bit right after it left her hand.

What the heck? Did they give her some self-homing magical spear?

I want that.

We hear a short scream, and Tess turns to me with a big smile on her face.

Yes, yes.

Did you level up? Sure seems like it. What the hell did you kill?

Good job, I guess.

After passing a few more meters, we get to her kill. It's an animal similar to a deer. Its leather is light brown in color, but what's weird are its slightly glowing antlers.

They are white and softly glow, slowly dimming, and finally stopping after a few more seconds.

There's no name glowing over the animal/monster, so it's dead.

Damn. I didn't even get to see its level.

"Deer Level 2," Tess whispers.

Oh.

"I leveled up, too. One point in mana and two into constitution."

Oh.

"I used my [Farsight] and [Psychokinesis], too."

Umm.

"I think we might be able to eat that." She points at the dead deer, and even though her face is back to a calm mask, I can see that cheeky little smile in her eyes.

Great, now she's leveling up, using her fancy skills, *and* finding us food? Isn't she too capable?

I glance at the dead animal and swear I can hear my stomach growling.

Okay, buddy, calm down. Soon!

Food, finally, about time!

I once again look at Tess, and she still has that barely noticeable yet cheeky look in her eyes.

Better be careful so I won't fall for her.

Yup. Everyone knows that love goes through the stomach.

Anyway, let's grab the deer quickly. I grab one leg and gesture to Tess to grab the other, and we quickly pull it back to the others.

Hadwin is keeping watch while Cassian and Dominic are waiting there, already done with their job.

Water and food, man. What more do you need? Fewer goblins would be nice, but I can't get too greedy!

"Cassian, grab the deer." I continue using my quiet voice.

"Damn," he whispers really quietly, but I can hear him.

Well, well, well, if it isn't the consequences of his behavior.

Tess takes the stuff from Cassian, and with Hadwin's help, Cassian hoists the deer onto his shoulders. The deer isn't that big, right?

He groans and bends his knees a little bit. There's a hint of anger in his eyes as he looks toward me.

Great, now use all this energy to carry the deer!

Oh, the joy of seeing Cassian struggle with the deer. I can't help but feel a bit smug watching him squirm under the weight of that animal.

Our way back is fairly uneventful, and when we get back to the clearing, Cassian is covered in sweat and breathing heavily. He drops the deer as soon as he can and then falls on the ground right next to the animal. His chest is moving up and down, and he is breathing with his mouth wide open.

Our "camp" seems fine, and people quickly surround us. They're excited, and I even see some smiles. Once again, I hear the dog barking, and this time, I look at him properly.

It's a fairly small, sandy-colored corgi causing a ruckus, barking away as his owner—a woman around fifty—pets him soothingly.

"It's okay, Biscuit. Calm down. Mommy is here."

I can't help but roll my eyes internally.

At least there is some wood close to the bus, so I guess they did do something.

Unfortunately, Damon's body is still at the end of the clearing. We will have to do something about it pretty soon, I guess.

"Oh no." The way Hadwin says it makes me grab the dagger, and I enter [Focus] while mana starts flowing through my body.

I hear a scream.

Tess gasps.

Everyone is looking in one direction.

Toward Damon's lifeless body.

My heart races with fear as I catch sight of the massive, hulking bear standing over him. Its thick, gray fur ripples with each heavy breath, and its piercing orange eyes glow like embers.

[Cinderbear - Level 19]

CHAPTER 20
CINDERBEAR

No one dares to move, not even a little bit. We just stand there and stare at the bear, just like a deer in headlights. Unable to move, unable to run.

We stand there and wait to get hit.

What makes it even worse is the fact that the bear is staring directly at me.

I don't dare move.

The Cinderbear sniffs in my direction once again and then turns his attention toward the body at his feet, then back at me.

After a few more seconds, the monster growls once.

I feel vibrations in my chest, and the few unbroken windows of the bus rumble. Some of them even break. But no one screams.

Total silence.

The monster then lowers its massive head and takes a bite of Damon's stomach.

Then it starts chewing while looking around.

A little bit of blood wets its maw, and then it bites once again, pulling one hand apart from Damon's body.

Crunch, crunch.

It eats slowly while looking around. At us, at the forest. For a second, it pauses and sniffs a few times. Again, toward us and toward the forest.

Another bite.

Crunch.

We just watch.

We are next, aren't we?

SPLAT.

Damon's head bursts open under the force of the bear's bite, creating a messy, wet sound.

The monster licks its teeth, and using both of its paws, it finishes the rest of the body.

A few people start crying as the bear stands up.

But that's just it. Its eyes land on me for a second, and then it turns around and leaves.

A few more seconds.

Then...

Screams, panic, crying. Everyone rushes back inside the bus. People push each other and scream as they rush in.

I am one of the first inside.

My hand trembles uncontrollably. Each breath I take is ragged and uneven as if I'm gasping for air in a vacuum. My heart pounds in my chest, a constant reminder of my terror.

My mind races with thoughts of what could happen next.

Will I survive? Is this the end?

Every noise, every movement, sends my nerves into overdrive. My senses are on high alert, and I keep mana flowing through my body.

The same feeling of helplessness and vulnerability washes over me like a wave.

I try to calm myself, steady my shaking hand, and regulate my breathing, but it feels impossible.

It takes a few hours before anyone dares to go outside. What a dumbass. Who would leave the bus with such a big fucking monster moving around?

And yup, that dumbass is me.

Tess was able to get to the roof of the bus with my help. Obviously, a few people followed her, as it felt like a safer place.

While Tess is keeping watch with her [Farsight], I move around.

Nothing. It's quiet.

The forest looks normal again. As normal as a forest can be after a few hours ago when the fucking Cinderbear came out of it.

It's strange how quickly things can change—from a source of nightmares to just another stretch of woodland.

But I know that I won't be forgetting what I saw anytime soon.

Even now, I feel scared while not letting it show.

Thankfully, Hadwin quickly joins me, and without saying a word, he fixes the mess I made of the would-be fireplace.

I thought I did a good job, but Hadwin totally demolishes it and starts over.

Hey, I'm a city boy, okay? My closest experience to camping is passing by a grill party in someone's garden.

Still, I watch carefully and try to remember as much as I can.

Hadwin lights the fire using a lighter he got from someone inside the bus, and after a few minutes, there is a crackling fire.

My primitive instincts instantly start lying to me.

You are safe. Fire equals safety.

Fire good.

What bullshit.

I help him, and we hang the deer against the side of the bus. Its hind legs are tied to the top frame of a broken window.

He is using a knife he got from me. I watch as he deftly slices away the deer's skin, working his way down from its hind legs to the front legs. The skin peels away with surprising ease, revealing the raw meat beneath.

Next, he guts the deer, carefully removing the internal organs and discarding them. The smell hits me, and I scrunch my nose, but I continue to watch and learn.

He works methodically, the knife flashing in the sunlight as he separates the organs from the meat. I can see the blood draining from the deer.

Once the deer is skinned and gutted, he begins to quarter the animal. I watch as he expertly navigates the cuts, making quick work of the process.

As he moves on to trimming the meat, I can see the precision in his movements.

So not a cop but a hunter?

He skillfully slices the meat; after each cut, he carefully sets the pieces of meat aside.

Meanwhile, we were able to boil water in an iron canister we brought back. Cassian and Dominic have already taken a few sips of the still slightly hot water, and I continue to monitor them while waiting for the water to cool down. They seem to be fine for now.

"Are you sure?" Dominic asks as Hadwin cuts the deer meat into smaller pieces. "We don't want that thing to come back after smelling it."

"It's not like we're inconspicuous here. A group of over twenty people is impossible not to notice. But we will use the canister." He nods toward the iron fuel canister we used to boil water in. "It shouldn't let off too much smell, and in our current situation, it's our best option."

I guess he doesn't want to scare people inside and deal with them telling him that animals will smell the meat if we cook it over the fire.

He turns back to me.

"They seem to be fine; the water should be safe."

I look at Dominic and Cassian. They really seem okay at the moment.

"How long will it take to cook a deer?"

"One to three hours."

I am hungry, but I'd rather be safe.

"Let's cook it for three hours, and if they are fine when the food is done, we can give it a try and drink some."

"Sure, for now, let's also put away some boiled water. We can let them eat a bit when the meat is done and wait a few more hours," Hadwin says.

Great, more waiting.

"Let's do that," I agree in the end.

I look at the duo for a second. They seem to be disturbed by our conversation.

Ungrateful pricks.

We put away a few bottles of boiled water, and the older man throws a lot of the meat into the canister and puts it on the fire. We also place a few pieces of clothing over the opening of the canister in hopes of filtering out the smell.

I also notice that Hadwin's fire isn't smoking that much, just a little bit of pale white smoke.

That's good.

We wait, and as we do, I continue to practice my [Mana Perception], but I can't get fully into it as my eyes keep glancing at the spot where the bear came from. Yet, after three hours, I at least get something.

I feel something from where Tess is.

She is practicing her skills, too, so maybe I can feel her using mana? It's as if, for a split second, I noticed something in the corner of my vision, but when I look there, I see nothing. A feeling like that.

Yet it's something.

I also get the same feeling from Sophie and Hadwin.

Hadwin is keeping watch while watching the fire, and Sophie...

Well, Sophie is talking to other people while keeping her sister close.

It's not that hard to guess what she is doing as my [Mana Perception] keeps getting a "feeling" from her.

At the start, I want to go there and stop her, to not allow her to slowly manipulate people to get on her side, but then I decide not to.

Most of the passengers are useless at the moment, and if she manipulates them, we might get at least something out of them.

The same way she manipulated Cassian and Dominic. Now I am sure of it.

Isn't her skill too powerful?

I am sure I can counter it somewhat because of my [Focus], and I have a theory that having higher mana helps, too, so I decide to invest all three points into it the next time I level up.

As for now, Sophie is avoiding Tess and Hadwin.

Tess, most likely because of me, and Hadwin because he's probably at a higher level than her.

Yet I am not naïve enough to believe that she won't try to control them if given an opportunity.

Once again, I think about stopping her, maybe even killing her, but quickly change my mind, and my suspicion grows.

To test it, I try something.

I think about hurting Cassian, and it's easy to imagine myself fighting him, hurting him. Yet when I try to do the same with Sophie, my mind wanders, and something makes me change my mind while looking for excuses to do so.

This can't be good, can it?

CHAPTER 21
WORST ENEMY

I am sure that there are some lingering effects of Sophie's skill. Unfortunately, I am unable to detect them at the moment. They seem to prevent me from hurting Sophie. They don't seem to affect me when I think about hurting someone else, so in the worst case, I can just blackmail Sophie.

That makes me reaffirm my decision to invest my next stat points into mana. I just don't know what else I can do, and my mind becomes a mess every time I think about it.

Sure, I can go and hurt her sister even now, but then what? Sophie will surely hate me, and I might be unable to fight back properly.

Should I ask Tess or Hadwin to do it?

It could work, but it might end up with her using them, or she may have already done so, and they won't be able to do anything about that.

So even though it deeply disgusts me, I need to give it a bit more time and learn more about how the skill works and what I can do to counter her.

Leveling up [Mana Perception] and [Mana Manipulation] should help me find what she did to me and counter it somehow. For now, it would be better to avoid her as much as I can.

After a few hours, Cassian and Dominic seem to be fine, so I drink plenty of water.

It smells and tastes slightly like gasoline.

That's another thing Cassian will have to pay for.

I know it's probably hard to wash it out properly, but he could try harder, right?

Still, I drink plenty and get some for Tess. After that, I grab one bottle and save it for later.

Obviously, there are a lot of people screaming and complaining, but I let Hadwin take care of that and move slightly away. No one bothers me, and I just filter out all the noises...

From the corner of my vision, I notice Biscuit the corgi eating small pieces of raw deer meat that fell from its carcass while Hadwin skinned it. The dog is trying to chew it, but the meat seems to be too firm for the small corgi to eat, so he just gulps it and runs toward the circle of complaining people while barking.

It looks like we have another tester besides our duo.

After a bit of complaining and worrying, they ate a few pieces of meat, so now we are waiting. If they are fine after a few hours, I will take some, too. I am sure that will start another round of complaining, but that's what Hadwin is for!

Yup. I will shamelessly eat some, save some for later, and disappear into the background.

Yup, again.

Tess will get a lot of it as well since it's her kill, and the rest isn't my problem.

Most likely, Hadwin will share some. It's not like we can put it into the fridge or plan to smoke it, so it's better if they eat it rather than throw it away.

I take a gulp of water, and Biscuit comes running to me. His owner, the older lady, is still complaining to other people.

Biscuit sniffs and barks softly while poking my leg with his snout. His tail swings wildly, but the tail is so short that it looks more as if he is shaking his butt. Like every corgi, he seems to be smiling cheekily.

Sigh...

I pour some water into the cupped palm of my hand and let him drink it. I repeat this a few times. Biscuit drinks everything and keeps licking my hand to get the last bits of water. Then, for a moment, he waits, and when he sees I am not pouring more, he barks, turns around, and runs back to his owner while barking at the people surrounding her. He wobbles from side to side as he runs because of his short legs.

We will have to go for water soon enough, but what if that bear is there?

Somehow, dying due to a lack of water doesn't sound that bad of an option.

After a few more hours, everything seems fine, so I eat plenty of meat. Because of our lack of seasoning, it tastes very bland, but it's food, so I eat as much as I think I can without making myself sick.

Tess gets her portion, and she shares some with a few kids.

Then another round of complaining starts.

As I sit by the bus and eat a few more pieces of meat, the corgi comes running to me and starts poking my leg with his snout.

Shameless little bugger.

With a sigh, I feed him a few small pieces of meat, and when he sees he won't get more, he runs back to his owner while barking.

It looks so similar to the last time that I wouldn't be surprised if I were in some kind of time loop.

Tess is still on the roof of the bus, keeping watch, and I keep feeling pulses of mana from her. My [Mana Perception] is now easier to use than before, so the pulses are clearer. I am sure she is training her [Psychokinesis].

Relying on her just a little bit, I practice my mana manipulation. Focusing on my legs, I keep sending mana into them. It's much more difficult than with my hands for some reason. Maybe because of the distance from my heart? I need to spend more mana to be able to reach my feet, but I keep pushing it. My intention is to use it to strengthen my legs. Maybe to be able to kick stronger or make me run faster?

To be honest, I don't know. It feels as if I am a monkey and someone put me inside the cabin of a helicopter and told me to fly.

It's annoying and discouraging.

But it's fun.

Every time I learn something, it feels as if it's worth it.

What excites me the most is the new skill I got from the past few hours of practicing. I did completely use up my mana a few times, and I still feel lightheaded, but I feel that it's well worth it.

[Oscillation].

The skill is still only at Level 1 and far from being useful in combat. Right now, I can use it while in deep [Focus], and the result is a tiny thread of mana extending from the tip of my finger. I am able to extend it a bit more than before and make it denser, and I am able to make it vibrate while testing. The result is an extremely sharp thread of mana.

During that, I also gain one mana stat point.

In the future, I hope to be able to apply [Oscillation] to weapons to make them sharper, but I am still far from that.

I stop my thoughts when Tess stands in front of me.

"The suns haven't moved at all since we came here."

That's also something I already noticed. We have been here for close to twelve hours, yet the suns are still in the same spot as when we arrived.

"Kevin said that there are some places in Alaska where the sun doesn't set for over two months, so maybe it's something like that?"

Maybe?

"Someone said that two suns so close to each other shouldn't be possible. The second one wouldn't be so

bright. Its brightness would be that of a bright star at most. Something about a binary star system."

I shrug.

"Also, I got my [Psychokinesis] to Level 2," she adds, and to prove it, two small stones float over the palm of her hand, spinning around each other.

"Did you try throwing stuff and pushing them with your skills to make them go faster?"

She nods.

"I'm not that proficient yet, and most of the time, it's worse than just throwing it, but I will get there."

"What about the others?"

She sighs shortly.

"Most of them are too stressed to even try something. Unsurprisingly, younger people seem to be getting into it a bit easier, but only a few were able to use their skills."

While we talk, her eyes keep moving around, still keeping watch.

"Kevin was able to use his [Reflection]. When you throw some small thing at him, he can reflect it back at you, but with much weaker force." The tiniest smile appears on her lips. "He says he can't wait for his Hero class."

Dude... What's with kids nowadays?

"I have a feeling that someone's trash-talking me!"

Tess sighs quietly and rolls her eyes a bit as a few school kids come closer to us. The boy leading them looks at me and smiles brightly.

"You must be the wulf slayer!"

Wulf?

"I expected you to be taller."

"You smell a bit."

"Kevin!" one of the girls shouts at him.

Is he asking for a beating?

"Anyway, nice to meet you." He reaches out with his hand, but I ignore it and continue sitting on the ground.

The same girl who yelled at him before pushes him back.

"W-we are sorry... Kevin is...weird sometimes." She ignores his outrage. Then she shyly smiles at me. "We wanted to thank you for"—she gestures around—"for everything, I guess."

Finally, some appreciation. Praise me more, bring me some offerings; sweets would be nice.

Darn, I would love some chocolate.

And sure, I may have done it all for myself, but they don't have to know. So I nod.

"At least introduce the others, Kevin." Tess shakes her head and starts pointing at people while introducing them.

Kevin Wilson, eighteen years old, with messy brown hair, the kid with a weird laugh.

Lily Chen, a petite seventeen-year-old girl, seems to be shy. Her black hair is tied in a ponytail.

Kim Min-Jae, a fifteen-year-old boy with big glasses. He is really thin.

"Others are keeping watch." Kevin smiles once again.

He seems to be really bright and optimistic. Already I don't like him and his seemingly endless energy.

My worst enemy, an extrovert. I already feel as if he is sucking the life out of me.

Is it a skill? It must be, right?

Tess probably notices my growing annoyance and stops Kevin, who is already talking about the class he would like to get.

Why Necromancer, and why does he think it will be OP? What happened to the Hero class?

Whatever.

"I wanted to show you something." Once again, he smiles. "Try throwing a stone at me," he challenges me.

So I grab a stone from the ground and throw it at him without any hesitation. I aim between his eyes. That surprises him a bit, but the stone comes close to hitting him and then flies back at me. The speed at which it flies back is much slower, and even the force seems to be weaker.

A cocky smile appears on his face, and then a second stone hits him right in the forehead.

"Fuuuuc..." He staggers back and starts rubbing his forehead while reproachfully staring at me.

Another stone hits his nether region.

"What the heck!" he screams in pain.

Deflect that, dipshit! Hahaha.

Look, he deserved that, and I am the last person to deny that I can be really petty sometimes.

"What was that for?" he asks, covering his crotch and looking at me like a sad puppy.

"I would recommend to you to practice a bit more."

The skill seems to be fairly useful, but it doesn't matter if the person controlling it is just a clown.

He sighs.

"You sound just like my dad. Practice more, Kevin. Use your brain, Kevin. Why are you so dumb, Kevin?" He gestures wildly and looks straight at me. "I will, I will, don't worry."

Something tells me that he isn't taking this whole situation too seriously.

Kim and Lily seem to be fairly scared. It's easy to see from the way they twitch sometimes and keep nervously glancing toward the forest, yet Kevin is... Well, I guess it must be slightly calming for other kids to be around him. It's his life, so you do you, Kevin.

"See ya later." He waves, and the others follow him. Kim nods toward me, and Lily gives me a small smile.

"I will go back to watch." I nod back at Tess as she says so.

"Buuurito, Buuurito, come here, boy," Kevin calls as they walk away from us.

"It's Biscuit. Miss Samantha won't like it if you keep calling him like that..." I hear Lily say.

Then they exit my hearing zone, and I get back to practicing.

CHAPTER 22
TROLL

In the end, Hadwin decides to smoke the rest of the meat. His reasoning is that the smell of meat wouldn't attract much more attention than a group of more than twenty people.

The bus and the clearing have become our base, and it looks like we can't go anywhere if we want to take the bus with us, as the clearing is surrounded by dense forest that's too thick for the bus to move through.

So we all wait for the end of the [Side Quest]. During that time, I drink some water, eat some meat, take a short nap on the floor inside the bus, and practice handling my skills and mana.

The suns, or whatever they are in the sky, do not move at all. For a whole twenty-four hours, not even a little bit. The weather is the same. The clouds look mostly the same. The wind is the same.

There is something deeply disturbing about that.

Then, a few minutes before the completion of the [Side Quest], a man stops in front of me.

"Ethan Lee," he introduces himself. He is ten or so years older than me, and his clothes are as neat as they can be in our situation. I notice a few luxury brands, and even his watch seems to be expensive.

"Greetings, Nathaniel, right? I couldn't help but notice your impressive skills, and you seem to be one of the few people with some balls on them. I'll be direct. I'm pretty affluent in the real world. I'm willing to compensate you for your assistance in keeping me safe. Of course, I understand if you have other priorities, but I think you'd be missing out on a valuable opportunity if you passed this up."

Uh? Okay? Is he for real?

Just out of curiosity, I ask, "How much?"

"Excuse me?"

"I am asking how much you are going to pay me."

"Oh, I see, straight to the point." He gives me a sly smile and fixes his clothes. "One million dollars," he says, as if it's something amazing.

I give him a moment, but he doesn't say anything else. *Dumbass.*

"What do you think will happen when we get back to Earth?" I ask.

"You've lost me there..."

One million dollars? What does he think will happen if we get back to Earth? Even right now, someone like Sophie would be worth tens of millions with her skill.

In five years? Just a handful of people could be enough to screw over entire nations.

One million. That's funny. Really.

"I am not interested." The conversation ends for me at this point, and I don't even listen to what he says. After

a minute, he just leaves, and I get back to counting down until the completion of the quest.

Side Quest completed.
Please choose one of the following rewards:
- *Flint and Steel Fire Starter*
- *Crossbow*
- *Short Sword*
- *Pouch of Dried Rations*
- *Portable Leather Flask*
- *Small Hand Shovel*
- *Cloak*
- *Mace*
- *Longbow*
- *Light Armor*
- *Leather Bracers*
- *Chainmail Hauberk*
- *Full Plate Armor*
- *Shield*
- *Spear*
- *Dagger*
- *Halberd*
- *Greataxe*
- *Greatsword*
- *Scale Armor*
- *Padded Armor*
- *Bedroll*
- *Clothes*
- *Waxed Canvas Tarp*
- *Sling*
- *Warhammer*

The list continues and is literally hundreds of items long without any categories, not even in alphabetical order—just a mess of random stuff.

Obviously, I have to scroll through all of them and see if there is anything more useful than what I want.

I go through the entire list, and in the end, it's still either a mace or a spear.

Since the start, I've wanted to pick a weapon, as everything else is useless if I'm not able to defend myself.

The spear might be more versatile and easier to master—I think. It can also be used for hunting or fishing, and for someone who doesn't have experience with weapons, it could be easier to handle than a mace. Another advantage is reach, but that could also be a disadvantage in a dense forest.

The mace, on the other hand, is more fight-focused and less versatile. Also, I would have to get close to the enemy to deal damage. Yet I like this option a bit more, as I should be able to deal much more damage just by swinging it like a bat, and it should be more durable without needing to sharpen the blade.

So, in the end, I pick the mace.

The weapon appears in front of me. No flash, no noise. It just appears on the ground right in front of me. One second, there's nothing, and then, even without me blinking, there's a mace on the grass.

I feel goose bumps all over my body. I even activated my [Focus] and [Mana Perception], but I didn't notice a thing.

One more thing I hate about this whole situation.

I bend down and pick up the mace.

The handle is made of sturdy wood. It is smooth to the touch, making it comfortable to grip. The head of the mace is made of iron, with menacing flanges protruding from it. The weight of the iron head feels substantial, making the mace feel heavy in my hand.

The entire mace feels balanced, making it maneuverable and easy to wield, even for someone like me who is inexperienced with such weapons.

Hmm, not bad. I think I like it overall.

I give it a few swings; it will take some time to get used to it, but it's doable.

Okay, let's check if we got a new side quest.

[Floor Quest]
Stay alive for 30 days.
Rewards:
- *Entrance to the second floor*
- *Access to Community*
- *1 skill point*
- *5 stat points*

[Side Quest]
Reach level 10.
Rewards:
- Trait of your choice

Huh? A trait? What could it be? I didn't notice anything like that before. Is it something new?

Also, what about classes?

Does "unavailable" mean that I don't fit the requirements to get one, or are they just straight-up unavailable to me in Hell Difficulty or on the first floor?

The longer we stay here, the more questions I have.

When I look around, I notice a short bow in Hadwin's hands. This decision surprises me slightly, as it seems like a dumb one.

Then I see a few other people bringing him stuff.

Short sword.

A shield.

Axe.

Ethan is one of the people giving Hadwin their gear.

Huh? Did he make some deal with all of them? And they agreed? How dumb are they?

Hadwin might be more ruthless than I thought.

To be honest, I might be disappointed I didn't come up with that by myself.

Tess and Sophie both got a spear. Kevin is already putting on some sort of armor.

So what now?

If things go the way the last twelve hours went, surviving one month doesn't seem that impossible. We already have a source of water, and we should be able to hunt a few more animals.

That's option one.

Option two is going into the forest with the purpose of leveling up.

The second option is much more dangerous, but there is also a chance that something will attack us even when we're not trying to level up. So just sitting here and trying to survive feels naïve to me. The safety we're feeling now is super unreliable and feels more like luck than something that is expected.

Soon after, I notice Hadwin and Sophie grouping up. Cassian and Dominic join them, and they slowly enter the forest.

Hadwin even looks toward me, and a small, apologetic smile appears on his lips. Then they're gone.

Well, there goes the neighborhood watch.

I don't want to sound too cocky, but they better be careful, going there without me. If this were a video game, I'd be mashing the quick-save button right now.

Also, did I just get ditched?

What the hell, Hadwin?!

Did Sophie get him as well, or was it his decision? Does he think he doesn't need me now when he's more geared up? Is his target becoming stronger than me? I don't like

it, not even a little bit. And what annoys me probably the most is that I somehow did expect Hadwin to organize everything and then come to ask me. Sure, I did want to rely on him while dealing with other people, but this?

Since when did I become so indecisive and come to rely on others to take the lead?

"Tess." I stop in front of a bunch of kids. "Are you going with me?"

I'm not in a good mood, so if she declines, I'm done with her.

That will be it, and I'll start a solo career as the world's least social adventurer. Sure, it will become more dangerous, but I can do it. If Sophie and Hadwin become stronger, I'll be at a disadvantage.

Tess just nods shortly and stands up.

"I'd like to take Kevin as well; I already gave him my old spear."

Kevin is standing there, wearing armor and holding her old spear. There's excitement visible on his face. It seems like they already talked about it.

"He'll have to listen to me. Did you explain it to him?"

"He will; we did talk about that, right?"

Kevin nods. This time, he seems to be a bit more serious.

We take a little bit of time to get ready.

"Let's go." I lead them toward the opposite side of the clearing where the others disappeared. I put my knife away, and I hold the mace in my right hand as we enter. My left hand is almost fully healed, so I feel confident.

Me at the front, Tess behind me, with Kevin at the last back; his main job this time is to leave marks for us so we won't get lost. At the start, I don't forget to control him a little bit, but he's doing it properly.

As always, I am surprised by how normal this forest looks, sounds, and smells as we enter deeper and deeper.

"Right side," Tess whispers after what feels like around thirty minutes of walking.

We all instantly slow down. "It looks like the deer we found last time," she continues, so I nod. "Deer Level 3."

"You can kill it."

I don't have enough range to hunt it, but Tess should be able to kill it from what I saw before, and some experience is good for her. With my [Mana Perception] activated, I watch as she throws her new spear. It flies much faster than it should. It also changes its trajectory a little bit as it leaves her hand.

With a scream, the deer falls to the ground. Dead.

Nice, get destroyed, Hadwin.

"Wait." Her voice is louder than before.

Rustling.

Stomping.

A tall figure moves away branches of trees and stops in front of the deer; it sniffs the deer and then looks right toward us.

> [Troll - Level 6]

It's a hulking mass of muscle standing three to four meters tall. Its long arms hang down, easily reaching the ground as it slouches menacingly. Dark, mottled skin stretches tightly over its massive frame, a grotesque display of raw power. Its monstrous face is a horrifying sight, with rows of massive teeth protruding from its twisted, gaping maw.

The troll's eyes, filled with a predatory hunger, stare right at us.

CHAPTER 23
BLOOD AND ANGER

My first instinct is to run away. The monster is easily twice my height, and its arms are abnormally long, reaching the ground. Its legs are a bit shorter, and it's slouching. Its mouth is full of long, sharp-looking teeth.

As I turn around, something makes me stop. Both Kevin and Tess are holding their spears, pointing them in the direction of the monster. Their stances are wide, and they are clearly ready to fight, even when the tips of their weapons are shaking slightly, especially Kevin's.

I clench my teeth.

Since when? Since when have I become like this?

I squeeze the weapon in my hand.

I kept thinking about running away; I did start relying on Hadwin, and I even waited for him to make the first move and take me with him.

What bullshit.

I hear another roar and stomping behind me.

It's fine if I am realistic and run away from fights I can't win, but why did I stop believing in myself and didn't even think about fighting the monster?

[Focus].

[Mana Manipulation].

[Mana Perception].

I activate all of my skills, and the world loses some of its colors as the mace in my hand creaks.

I am so pissed off, but up until now, I tried to hold it back.

Hadwin?

Goddamn asshole. I will beat him up for even thinking about messing with me.

Sophie? Just wait, there is a lot she has to pay for.

The Cinderbear?

Fuck you, you overgrown asshole.

I bury my leg into the soil, and the ground under my feet cracks slightly as I dash right against the attacking monster.

I focus more, and the world loses even more of its colors. Everything other than the troll seems blurry, and the sounds the troll makes seem louder.

Pain hits me as I use both of my hands to grab the mace.

The troll swings its right hand, and without any hesitation, I move to the right, closer to its body, and duck under its hand.

More mana.

My muscles complain from stress as I don't even try to save mana and let it wildly flow through my body.

Crunch.

I hit its knee with the mace. Together with a loud crack, it roars, and saliva flies out of its mouth.

The troll supports its weight by putting its hand on the ground, but I instantly lift the mace high into the air.

Crack.

The mace hits its arm.

Another roar and the monster's bloodshot eyes look at me.

I duck under its swinging left hand and hit its wounded knee once again.

It lets out a louder roar full of pain.

At the same time, a spear hits the side of its face, but it only scratches it slightly. I grab the falling spear from the air and throw it back where it came from.

Another swing, and I dodge again. Then the monster puts more weight onto its wounded knee and tries to charge me.

The charge is slow, and I carefully move behind the tree. The monster roars at me.

Then another spear hits him, this time on the back of the head. The troll roars and turns around.

Instantly, I move closer and, with full power, hit its other knee.

My muscles burn. My forearm hurts from aftershocks. The wound I made seems devastating, the mana strengthening my attacks beyond belief.

The troll turns back to me, and Tess quietly gets behind the troll.

Kevin helps and stabs the troll a few times. He isn't able to hurt it too much, but it makes the troll try to turn around while supporting its weight with its hands.

Crack.

I hit its unwounded hand as it tries to turn. It roars, full of pain and hate. Then the troll turns back to me again. It's

breathing wildly, drool is flowing from its mouth, and it keeps making biting moves with its mouth.

I hit its hand once again, and Tess and Kevin continue stabbing it from behind.

This time, the troll doesn't turn around and keeps staring at me with the eyes of a wild animal pushed into a corner.

Through my [Mana Perception], I feel Tess collecting a large amount of mana. Right after, her spear burrows itself deep into the back of the troll's neck, and blood starts flowing out of its mouth.

While trying to put some weight on its legs, the monster wobbles and falls down. It tries to support its weight with its arms, but it's unable to, and it falls face-first to the ground.

Waiting for that, I run more mana through my body and quickly step closer and hit the side of its head with as much power as I can muster.

Then again and again.

Blood splashes onto me, and its roar is almost deafening.

One of its arms partially hits me, and it throws me through the air.

I roll to reduce the impact and stand up.

The mace is still in my hand.

Tess grabs Kevin's spear and throws it at the troll with a push of her mana, and this time, it burrows deep into its eye.

The monster tries to stand up using its hands, but it's just flailing wildly, unable to do so.

While dodging its arms, I step closer and once again hit the side of its head.

Crack.

Its movements slow down, and the monster spasms a few times before powerlessly falling down.

> **[You have defeated a Troll – Level 6]**
> **[Level 3 > Level 4]**

Without thinking, I put all three of my stat points into mana.

I proceed to pull out both spears and throw them back to Tess and Kevin.

In the process, more blood lands on me: on my hands, my shirt, my face. But I just wipe it off with the palm of my hand.

"Use your stat points," I tell Kevin.

He nods.

"Already did so," says Tess.

I check the troll from up close, but there doesn't seem to be anything useful worth taking. So, instead of that, we move to the deer.

It's smaller than the one before, and we make Kevin carry it while taking short breaks once in a while.

When we get closer to the clearing, Tess notices something and stops us.

"Two goblins, Level 2 and 3, red tattoos," she whispers.

I don't like that at all.

They are too close to our base, and their tattoos are different.

"Level 3 is mine. You and Kevin take care of the other one," I say.

It's good for them to get as much practice as they can.

Kevin slowly puts his deer on the ground, and we sneak closer to the goblins. Tess leads us right into their path, and

we crouch behind the trees and bushes and wait for them to walk into us.

Let's see how you like it.

I still remember them doing a similar thing to us while being led by the goblin shaman and that goddamn wolf.

They slow down as they come closer, and I can hear them sniffing.

Without waiting any longer, I rush at them as a surprised scream escapes their mouths.

The Level 3 goblin stabs at me, but I dodge it and hit its head while strengthening my body. Its head explodes like a watermelon hit by a sledgehammer.

Pieces of bone and brain fly everywhere, and its headless body falls to the ground.

Heads up! Oh, wait...

Well, that's one way to blow someone's mind.

Not having anything else to do, I watch as Tess and Kevin fight against the other goblin armed with a spear.

Tess is holding back a little bit and letting Kevin fight the goblin, but every time it tries to charge him, she stabs at its leg.

At some point, Kevin uses his skill, and the goblin's attack bounces off him while he pushes closer, and his spear goes through the goblin's chest.

After a while, the green monster dies.

We then grab both spears, and Kevin once again puts the dead deer on his back.

"Ugh, why did I have to end up with Bambi on my back?!" the eighteen-year-old schoolkid complains, while struggling to maintain his balance as he carries the dead deer through the forest. "Seriously, though, can someone remind me why I'm the one doing this? I mean, I'm not even a certified deer-carrying expert!" He continues to

grumble playfully, trying to lighten the mood despite his obvious discomfort.

I mostly ignore his grumbling, and Tess is focused on keeping watch.

Her [Farsight] has proven itself really useful this time.

As we walk through the forest, I circulate mana through my body. Not a massive amount, just a little bit to get more used to it. I also use [Mana Perception] once in a while, but the only reaction I am getting is a weak pulse of mana from Tess.

In the end, we get safely back to the clearing. Before we enter, I stop them.

"Beginning now, try to avoid Sophie as much as you can. She has some skill that can influence people's feelings or make them feel what she wants."

Sure, I wanted to ignore what she does as she could make other people stand up and do something that isn't hiding inside the bus... That would also increase my chances of survival.

But now that they kicked me out of their club?

Fuck them.

I want to see them dealing with a bunch of angry people if it gets out.

"Tell others to be careful and don't let her touch you. It makes her skill stronger."

I am sure Tess will be careful, and I have a suspicion that Kevin's skill might counter hers if he levels it up.

[Reflection].

What would happen if he uses it while she is trying to influence or manipulate him?

"If Sophie talks to you, try using your skill," I say to Kevin.

"Who knew being a human mirror could come in handy, huh? So, no worries, my brain is staying off-limits!" He chuckles.

We enter the clearing. As we get closer, we find people once again huddled closer to the bus. There are a bunch of people surrounding someone.

I spot a haggard Hadwin, Sophie, and Dominic.

And Cassian?

He is sitting, his back against the wall, while they wrap a piece of cloth against a terrible wound.

His entire right arm is gone.

CHAPTER 24
THE PRICE OF HELP

Cassian's breathing is rough. He inhales sharply and quickly exhales as if trying to take in as much air as he can. His pupils are dilated, and he is shaking. Blood keeps flowing out of the terrible wound, and his skin is getting paler by the second.

The one most shocked by all of this is Dominic. The man is trying to squeeze the wound, tie something around it, doing everything he can to stop the bleeding. His hands are shaking almost as much as Cassian himself.

"Damn it, not like this..." He keeps pressing a piece of cloth against the wound. "Someone...do something!" he screams.

The only answer to his pleas is quiet mumbling and then silence.

After a while, Cassian loses consciousness.

"No, no, no, wake up, wake up." Dominic keeps shaking him. "Hadwin, help me, for God's sake. Sophie, you too." He turns to them, but his answer is only silence.

No one knows what to do.

"He's like this because he tried to protect you!" The rage is visible on his face as he turns toward Sophie. "So at least freaking say something!"

No answer, and she averts her face away from him.

"You bitch!" He rushes at her but quickly comes to a stop when Hadwin blocks his way.

"Dominic, you have to calm down. Acting like this won't help anyone." His voice is soft but firm.

"You...you..." Dominic clenches his fists, and I can almost hear his teeth grinding.

Then he swings his fist at Hadwin.

Unsurprisingly, it doesn't land.

Hadwin easily dodges it and hits Dominic's chest. Even I can see that he is not using his full force, yet Dominic flies back and falls to the ground.

"I'm sorry...but there's nothing any of us can do for him."

"Damn it..." Dominic just covers his eyes and stays lying on the ground.

"Damn it..." he adds again.

So they just stand there, and in a few minutes, Cassian's breathing stops. This time, his friend doesn't say anything, just stares at him. After a while, his gaze turns to Sophie. It's full of resentment. He just asks, in a quiet voice, for Hadwin and the others to help him bury his friend.

But at this point, I'm done listening.

I poke Kevin to make him come back to reality, and with his help, I hang the deer by its hind legs in the same place where Hadwin skinned the first one.

I stand there for a second and just stare at the deer while playing with the knife in my hand.

I still remember Hadwin doing it, so I should be able to do it somehow, but damn, I'm not happy about that.

Sigh.

Let's not waste more time.

I am about to make the first cut, but then I change my mind and decide to try something else. I use my new skill, [Oscillation], and a sharp, pointy shape of mana comes to existence on the top of my finger. Not waiting any longer, I make two cuts—one on the deer's neck to get rid of as much blood as I can and the other one on its belly, from its hind legs toward its front ones.

The mana at the top of my finger isn't as sharp as I would like it to be, so I enter [Focus] and activate [Mana Perception]. While feeling my own mana and watching its flow, I continue using [Mana Manipulation] to create a longer, sharper, and denser thread of mana.

Damn. Did it really take four skills to skin one deer?

I enter a deeper state of [Focus] and continue disassembling the deer. In the end, I don't even use the knife and just focus on improving my mana manipulation and getting used to [Oscillation] as much as I can.

It is hard to use so many skills at once, and the mana drain is pretty significant to the point where I am thankful I invested my stat points into the mana stat. When I finally run out of mana, I continue by using the knife.

Unfortunately, I didn't level up any of my skills, but I am sure I improved the way I was handling them. While doing so, I also got a few new ideas, so I hurry up with skinning the deer so I can get to testing them.

I step back when I am done and look at all the harvested meat. It could be worse.

Not bad at all.

"Fuck, that's brutal! Half of Bambi is still on his bones and the ground."

Fuck you, too, Kevin. Oh, and eat shit, Kevin.

"Hadwin did it much cleaner," Tess says.

Even you, Tess?

"Yeah, I guess we'll call it the 'half-Bambi special,'" Kevin continues.

You are so done...

"Hadwin's method was more 'fine dining,' while Nathaniel's"—Tess pauses—"is more 'post-apocalyptic buffet.'"

What does that even mean?

Kevin giggles. "It seems Nathaniel has taken a minimalist approach to skinning that deer."

I interrupt them before they can continue. "Hey, Kevin?"

He turns to me, curiosity visible on his face.

"Yes?" he asks.

"Take a few kids and smoke the meat. You saw Hadwin do it, so learn from that. If you fuck it up, I swear you will be eating smoked deer ass until we get out of here."

His pupils expand from surprise.

Reflect that, little twerp.

Then I turn to Tess, who is suspiciously on her way somewhere else, clearly much smarter than Kevin.

"Tess?" My voice is soft and creepy, even to myself.

She stops in the middle of her step and shudders. "Y-yes?" When she turns to me, she is trying to keep her face expressionless.

"You have two hours to get your Psychokinesis to Level 3."

"Ehm?!"

I leave her like that.

After around an hour, Hadwin comes to me while I am munching on some dried meat from the first deer and drinking some water. He waits until I finish and only then starts talking.

"Hey, I noticed you could use a few pointers when it comes to butchering a deer."

Oi, are you asking for a beating? Look, it was my first try. I will do much better next time.

Okay?

Okay.

"I wanted to talk with you about what happened." He finally gets to the reason he is talking to me. "We got attacked by a bunch of goblins. This time, they had red tattoos, and they had a goblin warrior with them. We didn't have a chance and had to run away."

Interesting. Why didn't they follow them?

But after looking at him, it seems like he wants to keep it to himself.

"We might have to go around to get to water or find another spot for it."

I just sit there and wait. There is no way I am going to make it easier for him. It feels so good.

Go for it. Ask me what you wanted to ask.

Come on.

"We should create a bigger group and try it again. We are almost out of water," he says.

Here. Just like that.

"We found plenty of trash bags, so we can transfer water in them," he continues, then looks at me. "I need your help."

Silence.

I take my time, actually enjoying torturing him like that. I know that he is a proud man, so asking someone less than half of his age for help must be painful.

After one minute, I finally give him my answer.

"I will help, but I want your handgun in exchange."

CHAPTER 25
GUN CONTROL

"**A**re you serious?"
"Yes."

Am I enjoying it too much? Who knows?

Hehe.

But Hadwin is the one at fault here. Who asked him to pick Mindblender Missy over me?

He sighs. "Can you even use it? It's not as easy as it looks."

"Yes, yes, no problem." *Just give it to me already; it's not like you have a choice.*

His brain is almost smoking as he tries to come up with a way around it. He doesn't like it at all, not even a little bit. But in the end, he sighs and slowly pulls out the weapon, offering it to me.

I shamelessly grab it. It's the first time I'm holding a handgun, and it's heavier than I thought it would be. It has a nice density to it and feels cold to the touch.

"So we have a deal?"

I nod in agreement. "Yes, we do."

Then I use [Oscillation] and cut the handgun apart. I make two swipes, and my mana cuts through the iron from Earth as if it's no denser than butter. After ensuring it's destroyed, I throw it into the forest as far as I can while strengthening myself with mana.

Hadwin's face is the funniest mix of shock and anger. He opens and closes his mouth as if he's a goldfish, and I swear I can see a vein popping up on his forehead.

Damn. He might attack me.

Wait. He might attack me?

Please do so!

You want to hit me, right? Just do it. If he does, I can mess him up, and later he would have to come back to me again, asking for forgiveness and for me to join him again.

Please, do it! Just one swing.

Unfortunately, he doesn't do it in the end.

"Why..." he barely manages to say.

"So, in one hour, yes? I will be taking Tess and Kevin; you can pick the others."

I leave without even answering, feeling much better than before our conversation. It's finally gone! Gun control on Floor 1 is truly excellent.

I feel as if a sword threatening to cut off my head has disappeared. The gun was the weapon I was most worried about. Other than that, I am sure no weapon any passenger has threatens me, and I am sure no one can beat me in a fight, not even if a few of them group up.

Now I just have to deal with Sophie, and the only danger will be monsters.

I can't even count how many times I shuddered when I heard Hadwin shooting his weapon. Every time, it could be a bullet going to the back of my head, and I wouldn't even be able to do anything about it, not at my current level.

I don't trust the man. He is too suspicious.

As for the gun's usefulness...who cares? My safety is the most important, and I am sure I can survive or run away even without the gun, even if I have to sacrifice a few people to do so.

Cinderbear doesn't count; fuck that guy.

"Tess, one more hour. Then we will go with Hadwin and a few others to bring back some water."

She just looks at me.

Leveling up her skill isn't going well, I guess.

"One hour," I repeat quietly.

Instantly, a small stone flies straight at my head, and I dodge it by tilting my head.

Pfff, try hard...

My [Mana Perception] senses a pulse of mana from Tess and then a smaller one behind me. I dodge to the side just in time to avoid the returning stone that lands back in Tess's hand.

At least pick a stone shaped like a boomerang if you want to do stuff like this.

I show her my thumbs-up and leave before she has a chance to react.

While walking away, I have a feeling that she's showing rude gestures right at my back. She wouldn't do that, right?

There's no way.

Yet I do not turn around to check and walk until I get back to Kevin, who is smoking some deer meat. There are three of his friends around him, and it's almost funny seeing them all trying to put together enough brain cells to deal with such a difficult chore.

"Hey, Nathaniel." Lily gives me a shy smile. Next to her is a Korean boy with big glasses. He just greets me by waving his hand.

"This is Jason," she introduces the blond boy.

"Sup," he says.

"Jason, help me out. Don't slack," Kevin complains and totally ignores me, so the boy just shrugs his shoulders helplessly and goes back to helping Kevin smoke the deer meat.

"Hey, Kevin." He slowly turns to me, and I can see that his face is slightly blackened from his attempts to smoke the deer.

Hehe, here we go.

"Oh deer, what a disaster! What happened here?" I say slowly and as emotionlessly as I can.

Shocked silence.

"Total grilltastrophe!" I try to add some emotions.

"Hey, do not..." Kevin starts.

"Such stag-gering incompetence!"

He stands up. "Listen here..."

I don't let him finish and hold my hand up. He pauses and looks at me while frowning.

"In one hour, we will go for some water. Me, Tess, Hadwin, and a few others. So be ready if you want to go."

I leave again. The third time escaping and leaving my opponents utterly defeated behind me.

Oh, and it's not like I spent an hour thinking of puns to say to Kevin.

Not at all.

Reflect that, you little twat.

One hour passes fairly quickly, and we group up. On one side, it's me, Tess, and Kevin; on the other, there's still slightly mad Hadwin; Sophie; a fit-looking, dark-skinned woman; and a tall man with ginger hair.

The woman is called Maya, and she is quick to tell us that she's a certified personal trainer.

The man is Leon, and he is built like a strongman. His accent is really strong, but I can't determine where he's from.

Hadwin has a bow, a huge knife, and an axe. Leon has a mace similar to mine, and Maya has a spear similar to Tess's.

Sophie is holding a small shield and a short sword.

"Tess will go first, and I will go right behind her."

She glances at me; I can see that she's somewhat nervous, but she agrees in the end.

Hadwin doesn't complain at all, only lifts one of his eyebrows and nods. Kevin ends up to my left, while Leon is to my right. The rest follow closely behind.

We get to the water and collect it without issue.

The forest is quiet.

We are on our way back when the forest grows even quieter, and I realize that the wind has stopped.

My breathing becomes ragged, and my body feels tense.

A minute passes.

We walk in total silence.

Two minutes pass.

Our steps and breathing sound so terribly loud.

A few more minutes.

My hand hurts from squeezing my mace's handle so hard.

A few more minutes.

I feel like vomiting.

More time passes.

The air feels so dry. All of us are breathing in loudly. It feels as if there isn't enough oxygen in the air.

Two minutes away from the clearing near the bus, one of the suns disappears. All of us start running as if we planned it.

A minute or so later, another sun disappears.

Total darkness. Not even a speck of light. Someone starts screaming, and then scratching sounds come from all around us.

I recognize goblins growling, and plenty of wolves start howling.

I hear a lot of trolls and some noises—I don't even want to know what makes them.

Someone begs for it to stop, and I can hear sobbing.

The cries of animals and monsters become louder and louder.

I hit something and fall down.

Mana is flowing through my veins, but I don't see anything, as if someone gouged out my eyes.

I just feel the mana all around me. From the ground, the sky.

I throw up. Such a monstrous amount of mana.

Then there is light.

The black sky is suddenly pierced by a bright light, which unfolds into multicolored bands reminiscent of polar lights. The greens, pinks, and blues move rhythmically, casting a dim glow that transforms the darkness into a scene resembling a muted morning.

Then we hear a bus horn and the screams of goblins and people from the clearing.

CHAPTER 26
GOBLIN WARRIOR

"Izzy!" Sophie screams and runs to the bus. We follow behind her, just not as enthusiastically.

The bus horn keeps sounding, and the screams of goblins become louder and louder.

We exit the trees and see other passengers inside the bus. Most of them...

There are two bodies outside, and a few goblins keep stabbing their bodies while screaming. One of them is even taking a bite out of them.

Then there is another group of goblins surrounding the bus. They laugh and growl, still outside, as people inside keep poking out with sharpened sticks and weapons they got from the quest.

Sophie staggers onto the clearing.

"N-no..." She stops, seeing around thirty goblins in the clearing. Most of them are Level 2 or 3, but some are Level 5 goblin warriors.

"Izzy..." she calls quietly, but some of the goblins already turn to her.

A pulse of mana extends from her body to the surrounding area. The goblins that turned to her look confused and turn back to the bus.

Another pulse of mana washes over the entire clearing. Even I feel something telling me to run away. Some goblins start to leave, but others poke them, growl at them, and they start looking and sniffing.

In between screaming voices, I hear that of a little girl; Sophie's face is deathly pale.

"Please..." She turns toward us. Another pulse of mana from Sophie, and I stop Tess and Kevin from taking a step toward the clearing.

They shake their heads, confused.

Hadwin seems to resist, but Maya and Leon slowly move a step closer and then stop. Even Sophie's skill is not yet strong enough to make them risk their lives.

The girl's eyes then turn to me.

Not to Hadwin.

To me.

"Please, Nathaniel, please..." Her voice breaks. Now, I don't feel any mana from her.

Is it doable? I look at the clearing.

Hmm.

I think it is. I can do it.

"Use your skill to make a few goblins come here. Around five."

I squeeze my mace and step closer to her.

I see her biting her lips, but she nods. She most likely wants us to rush straight to the bus, but that's too risky.

It's harder to run that way in case something happens.

"Tess, save your mana as much as possible. Only throw your main spear at Level 5 goblins and only if needed."

Not wasting my mana anymore on [Mana Perception] or any other skill, I step a bit back, just far enough into the forest so not all goblins will spot us. Sophie most likely uses her skill, as six goblins turn, screeching, and rush toward us.

I breathe out.

Four Level 2 and two Level 3.

I breathe in.

With her spear, Sophie stabs the first goblin that rushes at us. The monster dodges it slightly and rushes closer to her, where it's hit with Hadwin's axe.

Tess attacks another one with much greater success, her spear stabbing its neck.

I surprise the goblin chasing me, aiming my mace at his face, but he lifts up his hand to block it. The mace breaks, and the goblin falls down screaming.

Another one comes at me. I step back, grab its spear, and make it lose its balance. Finally, I smash his head with my mace while he is staggering.

I notice Leon and Maya finishing off the first goblin I attacked.

Another one attacks me from the side, wildly swinging his dagger. And yet another one tries to hit Tess while she is still fighting the first one.

I strengthen my body with a little bit of mana and throw my mace, hitting the goblin that is attacking Tess. I'm able to distract him enough so she can defend herself.

I dodge the goblin's knife and pull out mine, stabbing it into the monster's back.

"That's all? You're just going to sit there because you feel tired?"

I step closer to her.

"You will stop only because your head hurts a bit?" I give her a cold smile and whisper, so only she can hear, "But it's okay, just lie down, and we can watch."

Her eyes become colder and colder with every word I say. More blood starts flowing from her bitten lips, and then she turns toward the clearing.

"You are such a bastard..."

With a groan, she falls to her knees and becomes paler and paler. More blood starts flowing from her nose and drips from her chin onto the front of her shirt.

Then the goblin warrior turns its gaze toward us. He bares his teeth and moves closer, followed by a few more goblins.

"Tess, you take the one on the left. Hadwin, shoot the goblin warrior just a little bit before we start, and then take one. Leon and Maya, the last one is yours. Feel free to run if you want to, but if you do, don't bother coming back."

I step toward the goblin warrior and lower my stance. The goblin does the same.

He is slightly taller than the other goblins and slim. The tattoos that cover his skin are in a much darker shade of blue.

He rushes at me, and in the middle of that, an arrow scratches his arm. Another arrow completely misses him, and then the others start fighting their goblins.

Unsurprisingly, even a Level 5 goblin is an amateur at best. His swings are faster and carry more force behind them. They are easier to read now that I've seen their fighting style and taken their unnatural speed and force into consideration.

I dodge the first swing. I dodge the second swing.

He growls, annoyed, and swings again, this time putting more force behind the swing. He loses a bit of balance when he misses, so I kick his leg, making him stagger even more.

I send just a little bit of mana through my body and swing downward with my mace.

He moves faster than before and is able to block it with his hand. It doesn't break. There is a wound on it, it's bleeding, but it doesn't break.

He bares his teeth as if smiling, so I take a quick step back and kick right his face with the bottom of my feet. I feel a crunch when his nose breaks.

Another loud roar, and he rushes me again, this time moving faster and using his hands to move while still holding the axe.

His face is a bloodied mask of rage.

[Focus].

The world becomes quieter. Under the polar lights, I focus on the goblin only.

He puts more strength into his left. I have already moved to the side by the time he jumps through the air, letting go of his axe. I feel mana from his hands as he reaches for me.

But I am not there.

More mana flows through my veins, and the mace's handle creaks in my hands. I wait until he misses me before throwing my mace, full power, at the goblin's back.

Crack.

The green monster lands and tries to turn to me but instantly falls, losing all power in its legs. He roars and growls, but his legs do not move at all.

With a hateful look in his eyes, he starts crawling toward me with surprising speed. I leap a back few steps.

I hold his axe in my hand. Before he gets to me, I throw it at him, using some mana. He covers his face, so the axe wounds him just a little bit.

What a terrible throw.

But when he pulls his hands from his face, I am already in front of him. My mace hits his head with full power. He desperately tries to cover his face with his hands, but it's too late.

Crack.

Crack.

Splat.

He finally stops moving.

> [You have defeated a Goblin Warrior – Level 5]
> [Level 4 > Level 5]

I instantly put all three stat points into mana, making it my highest stat.

> [Name: Nathaniel Gwyn]
> **Difficulty:** Hell
> **Floor:** 1
> **Time left until forced return:** 4y 363d 18h 9m 59s
>
> **Level:** 5
> **Strength:** 7
> **Dexterity:** 9
> **Constitution:** 10
>
> **Mana:** 11
> [Primary Class: Unavailable]
> [Subclass: Unavailable]

Skills:
Focus - Level 3
Mana Manipulation - Level 3
Mana Perception - Level 2
Oscillation - Level 1

[Skill Points: 0]
[Stat Points: 0]

Chapter 27
Moving Forward

I get back to the others just in time to see Sophie collapse to the ground.

"I...I can't anymore..." Her voice cuts off, and the goblins that had been ignoring us up until now start looking around confusedly, most likely wondering where their friends went.

I stare at Sophie for a moment, but it looks like that's all I can get from her.

"Hey..." My voice spreads through the clearing, louder than it should be and distorted but recognizable as mine. All thanks to the mana I sent to my throat and vocal cords.

"You have ten seconds; if you stay inside and don't attack the goblins after the time passes, we will leave." My voice is cold, and I mean every word I say.

"You can't..." Sophie barely gets out, supporting her body with her arm to look up at me.

But she doesn't use her skill on me. She knows that would be it, and I would just leave her sister and the others

if I sensed even a hint of her mana trying to manipulate me.

This time, I will decide on my own, and if I put myself in danger, it's only because I am sure I can survive it and gain something out of it.

The goblins screech and sniff and slowly turn toward the sound of my voice.

Even if they rush us now, I am sure I can run away pretty easily.

If they don't attack them, I will leave. I won't risk my life just for them to sit on their asses.

"Five..." My voice spreads through the clearing, and goblins start slowly moving toward us, ignoring the bus and its passengers.

"Four."

Two goblin warriors poke and push a few other goblins, making them more aggressive.

"Three."

One of the goblin warriors is Level 6. He holds a dagger in each of his hands; the other one is Level 5 and holds a spear.

"Two."

Their backs are turned to the bus, and they are halfway to us, leaving two half-eaten bodies behind them.

"One."

My voice is louder and sounds more like me as I keep improving my usage of mana.

> [Mana Manipulation - Level 3 > Mana Manipulation - Level 4]

The doors of the bus open, and an older man, the bus driver—I think Jacob is his name—hurries out, waving

an axe in his hand. His voice is weak and shaky, but he is attacking. Right behind him, a few more people attack, forcing some of the goblins to turn around and deal with them.

For a second, the thought of running away goes through my mind. As they distract the goblins, I would get at least a few more minutes to run without being pursued.

But shouldn't you run only if you are sure you can't win?

I step toward the attacking goblins and enter [Focus]. All useless noises become filtered out. Some colors lose their vibrancy, yet some become that much more vibrant—the color of blood, polar lights on an inky dark sky.

"Sophie, make the goblin warriors focus on me."

I saw them fighting; none of the people could deal with them, especially if the goblins attacked in multiples.

"Tess, you will stay here and support others with ranged attacks. Use spears from dead goblins."

They are already so close.

"Kevin, you will be on the front line with Leon and Hadwin, and Maya will support you."

I am surprisingly calm.

Around twelve goblins are rushing at us, and I see around five of them fighting with other passengers. Goblin warriors stay slightly in the back, and I dash toward them while strengthening my body, right through a group of Level 2 and 3 goblins.

I swing.

A head explodes like a watermelon.

[You have defeated a Goblin - Level 3]

Another swing.

[You have defeated a Goblin - Level 2]

Multiple goblins attack me, but I put more force into my legs and jump right over them while still running.

There are two goblins slightly behind and surprised to see me.

[You have defeated a Goblin - Level 2]
[You have defeated a Goblin - Level 2]

Then I stand up in front of two goblin warriors. I feel a pulse of Sophie's mana from behind me, and other goblins rush at them instead of turning back.

There are only six of them, so good luck.

Mana rages through my body, and I enter deeper and deeper [Focus].

[Focus - Level 3 > Focus - Level 4]

Breathe out.

The world becomes quieter, and I see only two opponents in front of me.

Breathe in.

I bounce on the balls of my feet and roll my shoulders back, a series of satisfying pops echoing.

Mana flares out, and I stomp my feet, feeling the earth respond beneath me.

The Level 6 goblin dashes and, in a split second, reaches me with both of his daggers stabbing toward me. There is blood visible on his teeth.

Before he reaches me, I also dash toward him and swing my mace as if it's a bat. At the last moment, he

pulls his daggers back and blocks my attack, sending him staggering backward.

I step back, almost breaking my ankles from the pressure I put on them. A spear stabs through the place where my head was. I already hold my mace in my right hand, and I grab a dagger with my left before I start dodging the attack.

I send more mana through my body and feel the muscles in my left shoulder and waist tearing from the speed of the movement as I turn my body and stab the dagger right into the goblin's left eye.

He tries to dodge but is unable to stop the inertia from his stab with a spear.

Then I jump to the side to keep the goblin warrior with the spear between me and the Level 6 goblin. Just in time, two daggers stab the body of the dying goblin.

Both of them growl, one of them from pain, the other one from annoyance.

Before he pulls his daggers out, I swing my mace at his head, holding it only in my right hand. He ducks and pulls his daggers out, so I quickly twist my body and kick his face. From the pain I am feeling, I probably cracked my shin.

The goblin is able to leave a cut mark on my leg as he flies backward.

Before he gets a chance to fight back, I put more strength into my legs and dash at him. In my mind, I scream from pain.

My mace hits his hand, and one dagger falls down.

He dashes at me, and I kick the bottom of his chin in exchange for a long cut on my left hand. The hand that already has torn muscles.

The goblin wobbles a little bit from the kick, and a spear comes flying out of nowhere and stabs through his right hand.

Nice one, Tess.

The last dagger falls down, and I kick against him as he dashes at me with the spear still stuck in his hand. He drops down, and I swing my mace downward, using enough mana to make my muscles hurt.

His face deforms under the mace.

One more hit to the same place.

His leg keeps twitching, and foam forms around his mouth.

The last hit.

> [You have defeated a Goblin Warrior - Level 6]

I turn around, take a few steps, and hit the conscious goblin on his head.

Once.

Twice.

> [You have defeated a Goblin Warrior - Level 5]
> [Level 5 > Level 6]

I put all stat points into mana and turn toward the bus. Just a few more.

CHAPTER 28
A WEIRD THING TO SAY

When I reach the bus, only three goblins are left alive. I hit the head of the goblin that is fighting with Jacob. He is the bravest one of the bunch, so I don't mind helping him first.

I dent the goblin's head, and he falls down, twitching and screeching. I step on his neck, and something cracks.

[You have defeated a Goblin - Level 3]

Another goblin is about to attack an older lady when her corgi's sharp teeth sink into its leg, halting its swing.

Good boy, Biscuit!

I see that the goblin is about to kick the brave dog, so I dash and hit the goblin's head. This time, I use mana, and his head explodes.

Hmm, am I getting too predictable?

Anyway.

> **[You have defeated a Goblin - Level 2]**

After that, I finish off the goblin that is kept at bay by Lily and a few kids who keep poking their spears and sticks at him so he can't get closer.

> **[You have defeated a Goblin - Level 2]**

That went pretty well, all things considered.

Jacob and a few other people look severely wounded, but the only corpses are the ones I saw at the start. A few people are still inside the bus, so I make sure to remember their faces. On the other side of the clearing, everything seems to have gone well.

Tess is not wounded, Hadwin also seems fine, but Kevin's armor is dented. Sophie, on the other hand, appears unconscious, and I would swear that Leon is missing one or two fingers.

I check my status and don't find anything new, so I look up at the sky once again.

The sky is inky dark with no stars at all. The only sources of light are the bright green, blue, and pink lights that swirl slowly in the sky, reminding me of polar lights, just much bigger and brighter.

I find it really beautiful.

The colors and movement are mesmerizing and provide enough light for us to see. The light is at the level of a dim morning, but it's much better than the pitch-dark darkness we went through just a few minutes ago.

But...

WHAT THE HECK?

How do you even get rid of two suns?

Anyway, it's almost certain that the suns we saw were fake, yet I can't even begin to imagine what is actually going on.

A fake sky and some kind of projection?

I guess it could be. We just started to learn to use mana, and from looking at all kinds of skills, mana seems fairly versatile.

Tess comes closer. "Nathaniel..."

Darn, I didn't even notice that I started spacing out while thinking about all of that.

"I'm out of cigarettes."

Well, that must suck.

But what a weird thing to say at a moment like this. Just say what you wanted to say.

She slowly breathes in, a hint of emotion visible on her face.

"Jason and Miss Miranda died. Leon lost a finger, and there are many wounded people..."

I see. So? I didn't know them at all, so there is no way I am going to mourn their deaths. She should know that.

Tess pauses for a long moment and looks at me as if trying to read my mind. She shifts slightly on her feet.

"Never mind, I'll keep watch..."

Nice! Now, let's talk with Sophie.

She is already back and inside the bus, her sister next to her. She's awake but still looking really tired. There's a lot of dried blood on her lips, chin, and under her nose. Her sister keeps crying while Sophie caresses her hair.

A few people step away as I walk in and stop in front of her.

"Let's talk."

Sophie hesitates for a moment but then slowly stands up.

Her voice is soft as she whispers to her little sister. "Wait here for me, Izzy."

We walk outside, just far enough away so other people won't be able to hear, and then we start talking.

"Name of your skill?"

"Manipulation," she answers instantly.

"Your level and level of skill?"

"I am Level 3, and the skill is also Level 3."

"Your second skill?"

"Mana Infusion."

Huh, what a weird name.

"Explain."

And she does so. It looks like her manipulation is what I thought it was. She can manipulate the emotions of other people, monsters, and animals. She can make emotions stronger or weaker, and if she spends enough mana or gets to touch her target, she can instill a feeling that the person didn't initially have.

Her other skill allows her to infuse mana into living beings and objects. She doesn't know what it does, for now, other than wasting her mana. It could strengthen some items or share her mana with others, maybe?

What's most interesting is that she started on the first floor with her manipulation at Level 2 and her mana with three stat points.

What the heck?

Even the system is playing favorites?

I did get [Focus], which only allows me to...well, focus. Damn.

I want [Manipulation] or [Psychokinesis], too. Even [Reflection] seems to be cool as heck.

Anyway, the system is clearly playing favorites.

I also want to ask Sophie what she did to me, so I can't even think about killing her, but I decide against it. During our whole conversation, I came to the conclusion that she doesn't even know about that, so it might be better not to let her know that I can't do much against her.

Before I leave, I get a promise from her that she won't try to manipulate me or people around me.

My kids, my underlings, my minions.

My meatsmokers, my biological binoculars.

Obviously, I don't believe her that much, but it should at least make her think twice, especially now when I can feel her using mana.

And that's it.

That's what I get for saving her sister, and we are now back to a cold war.

CHAPTER 29
IMPORTANCE OF MANA

Much later, all of us are either inside the bus sleeping or gathered around the fairly large campfire we set up, as it's not only darker now but also colder. It's not too cold, but it's noticeable.

We've dragged all the dead goblins to the edge of the forest, perhaps in hopes that the Cinderbear will eat them and leave us alone in case he comes back. We've also fortified our position somewhat.

To be honest, it's pretty makeshift, but I guess it's better than nothing. There are sharp sticks planted in the ground, pointing toward the forest. Some of them are quite long, while others are really short, possibly intended for goblins to step on.

We've also slightly upgraded the bus with pieces of wood that replace some windows and reinforce the entrance. It's rather unsightly and took a long time to complete.

A few small groups of goblins came while we were working, but they were relatively easy to deal with. They

consisted of only two to four goblins, all of them Level 2 or 3.

So now, we just sit here. The fire crackles pleasantly, and the warmth feels nice on our skin. Oddly, the flames are redder than they should be—just another strange occurrence. At this point, I wouldn't even be surprised if the flames shone like a rainbow.

I'm sitting on the ground, and nestled between my legs is a small corgi. Well, it's not that small, to be honest; it's quite heavy and probably ten to twenty percent bigger than before.

Surprisingly, this little doggo has taken a liking to me after I fed it a few times and saved it from a goblin.

Time to pay!

I boop its snout, and the corgi woofs in its sleep, mostly ignoring me.

Now that I look at it up closely, he really does resemble a burrito. Maybe Kevin isn't that far off at this point.

As for the corgi's owner? Well, she isn't happy about it, but she doesn't say anything—at least not to my face, obviously. I'm sure she isn't so quiet behind my back.

But, darn it, Biscuit. You're heartless.

Good boy!

What did she do to you? Did she try to turn you into a vegan or something?

I boop his snout once more; it's cold, and the doggo only scrunches its face this time.

Tess is keeping watch again, along with Sophie and her sister. All three sit on the roof of the bus while a few more people keep watch from inside. We didn't ask them to; they're just that worried.

It's easy to notice how close everyone is to each other as if seeking safety and warmth from the people around them.

Perhaps a bit too close? A little closer and Kevin will end up sitting on my lap—well, on Biscuit and then on my lap. I'm sure the bravest doggo of the first floor of Hell Difficulty wouldn't take that lying down.

On my other side is Lily. Like many people, she also leveled up and used her stat points. It seems that the experience requirements to level up from Level 0 to Level 1 are incredibly low. People were able to level up even after only poking a goblin once with a stick.

Oh, and one more thing. I've noticed that my emotions are somewhat subdued. The reason is most likely [Focus]. I finally realized that I'm maintaining a lower version of the skill almost constantly and only enter a deeper state when I want to. Has it almost become a passive skill?

It's hard to explain, and I'll need to experiment a lot more to fully understand it, but some of my emotions, such as fear, anxiety, and desperation, are still present— just much weaker than they should be. [Focus] is, well, allowing me to focus on my survival, and either I'm doing it on my own and unconsciously, or it's part of the skill.

That would explain a lot.

Sure, I'm a pragmatic person, but even in situations like this?

Absolutely not.

So yeah, thanks, Mr. Focus!

I should be more concerned about having some of my emotions nearly erased, but if it's for survival, I really don't mind losing a few. As for what will happen to me after I level up [Focus] even more? That's a problem for tomorrow's me!

Thank you for your service, future Nathaniel.

I continue to use my skills and listen to the conversation of people around the campfire.

"Noticed it even before we got there. There were some disappearances of people all around the world. I heard that an entire class of kids disappeared in Japan a few weeks ago, and another day, a plane full of passengers."

Oh?

"I heard it, too, from my mom. Her friend said some people on the beach disappeared. She saw it with her own eyes. One moment they were there, and then they just vanished. Plus, a lot of animals started going wild lately, attacking people and stuff. Didn't they also spot super big wolves?"

Huh, am I the only one who didn't notice anything? Well, who watches the news nowadays, right? And it's not like I need a friend to hear such stuff from them. Yup, I'm not the odd one here.

"I thought it was just a bunch of nonsense. They didn't even show it on the news. Just a few clickbait titles on websites. Some explosions in cities and terrorist attacks. Plenty of weird rumors..."

"So do you think we're not the only ones on the first floor? There might be some people who came here before us?"

"Maybe? You saw the rewards, right? One of them is Community, so maybe we'll be able to talk to others."

"Maybe we can create guilds!" Kim says.

A moment of silence, then they continue, completely ignoring the boy.

"There might be other difficulties other than Hell. If so, why did we end up here?" Hadwin looks around, and no

one can answer. "Also, what will happen after we get back to Earth?"

Not after, Hadwin, IF. I don't want to be mean, but it doesn't look like most of us will make it.

"Can you imagine the mess it will create if a bunch of superhumans appear out of nowhere?"

Who cares? That's tomorrow Nathaniel's problem!

Maybe not even his; that's the government's problem! Finally, they will do something useful with my taxes.

"And we just started. Look at how strong we are after just a little over one day," Hadwin says.

A few eyes turn to me.

Darn, stop, I'll blush.

But during Hadwin's entire speech, I notice that he isn't too unhappy. It's hard to catch, but I swear I hear a hint of satisfaction and relief in his voice.

"How many floors do you think are here, Mr. Hadwin?" Lily asks quietly, and a few heads turn to the older man.

"I want to know that, too. Also, do we have to move to another floor, or can we spend the entire five years on the first floor? That's something we'll have to think about. Other floors might be much more difficult, so staying here might be a good idea."

A few people nod. They continue theorizing, but most of the time, they don't say anything interesting, so I just filter it out. After some time, they begin talking about what everyone likes to talk about—themselves.

"I'm pretty well-off back on Earth, and I know some powerful people, so if we get back, I can arrange something for us. Imagine how much we can get paid with skills like this."

Oh, come on, shut up, Ethan.

"What if we won't be able to use our skills after we get back to Earth? What if all of this disappears?" Kevin says.

Huh? Good one, Kevin. It doesn't sound too impossible.

The group around the crackling fireplace quiets down, everyone deep in their thoughts.

I look up at the beautiful lights in the sky. What would I do? I don't like the thought of losing mana.

To be honest, I hate it.

I let it flow through my body, pushing it, making it circulate faster and slower as I wish. Wisps of mana appear on the tips of my fingers, like smoke, but then they become denser, sharper, and longer when I want them to.

That's another problem for tomorrow's me.

But I have a suspicion that tomorrow's me would prefer staying over returning to Earth without mana.

CHAPTER 30
DEATH IN A DISTANT LAND

Fantastic. The phony "suns" have returned to grace us with their presence.

They just appeared out of nowhere and totally blinded us after a day in darkness, brightened only by beautiful polar lights.

The sky looks exactly like the sky we saw the moment we entered the first floor of this godforsaken Hell Difficulty something.

Before that happened, we had to deal with one more attack of fifteen or so goblins led by a goblin shaman. The Level 5 jerk died like he wasn't even trying.

The goblin shaman got sniped by Tess even before he was able to do anything. He just entered the clearing, and an unnaturally fast-flying spear—or should I call it a homing missile at this point?—went straight through his chest and pinned him to the ground.

Look, I love my [Focus], I really do, but what the heck! Whose ass do I have to kiss to get it as well?

I see that Tess is trying not to act smug about it, but it's making it even worse.

As a consolation prize, I was able to level up my [Oscillation] to Level 2. It sure is hard to level up. Most likely because of how OP it is, right?

RIGHT?

So anyway, during the fight, I caught a few goblins alive.

Well, I broke their legs and hands, so they couldn't do anything.

I totally don't understand why that made some people slightly sick and look at me like that. I did it for them! So they could stab defenseless monsters with their spears to get some experience. It's not like I can gain much from Level 2 creatures anymore.

They should praise me, not look at me like that.

Also, give me some chocolate. Damn, I would kill for some sweets right now.

I was able to obtain a candy drop from Lily—she had saved one for later but was nice enough to give it to me.

In exchange, I gave her two bloodied Level 3 goblins to finish up.

YES, I know, I know.

The candy is much more valuable and harder to come by than these green jerks. But I'll pay more, no worries.

Lily didn't seem to like it as much as I hoped, but that's something to be expected. She seems too nice for a place like this.

Another thing is Biscuit.

The little doggo has grown a bit. His proportions are mostly the same, but he is slightly bigger. It might be the monster meat he ate, or maybe the little doggo is leveling up.

I swear, if he also gets an OP skill, I will be so angry.

He's also becoming smarter every day. He already knows when I'm going to eat and sniffs around with big, sad eyes that become super cheeky the moment I give him some food.

Shameless little bugger.

We were able to get some water once more, and Hadwin hunted a boar on his own and brought it back. The animal must have weighed twice as much as him, but he brought it back alone.

In comparison to the first day or so, this seems too easy.

This thing is called Hell Difficulty, you know. It's not like I'm complaining that we're not getting eaten.

It just feels like the calm before the storm, so I stock up. I put plenty of food and a few bottles of boiled water inside my gym bag and place it somewhere easy to reach, so I can grab it and run if needed.

I notice a few other people are doing the same.

It's still difficult; we have to fight, hunt our food, fight for water, but...this is Hell Difficulty.

There are such monsters as the Cinderbear, and seriously, fuck that guy.

Obviously, there is some infighting. Dominic still hates Sophie, and Hadwin as well, because the older man is defending her.

Oh, and one more person died from wounds she got during the fight with thirty goblins. Lily told me with red eyes that her name was Ava. It looks like she was fairly nice to the kids, so the girl seems to be sad about that.

As for me, I'm surprised that more people didn't die and that more and more of them are asking us to bring them with us when we go hunting or for water.

Once again, Kevin kept trashing them behind their backs, calling them leeches and saying he won't be power-leveling them, something about the bus and grinding.

As most of the time, I ignore him.

Even now, I have a suspicion that he has some life-drain skill. Every time he starts talking so excitedly, I feel as if he is sucking energy out of me.

It has to be a skill.

Tess always steps in and stops Kevin from talking. It's nice to have someone to deal with people like him.

I'm not ungrateful, so I teach her in my free time. She was able to obtain [Mana Manipulation] as well and is now teaching it to others. It's interesting to watch as her version of the skill is slightly different from mine. How to say it... It seems like she is relying on the skill itself more than I am. In my case, I'm trying to "feel" it on my own a bit more, instead of just activating it through the system.

Anyway, it's nice to have another test subject, and to make Kevin a bit more useful, I make him train his [Reflection] while I watch him with my [Mana Perception].

His skill seems to be amazing for defense, so I'm trying to copy it. I keep watching the movement of his mana while he uses it. There are no results after hours of trying, but I'm sure I will come up with something if given enough time.

Everyone is practicing as if their lives depend on it. They're swinging, stabbing their weapons, practicing their skills, and complaining.

A lot of complaining.

I wouldn't believe how entitled some people are, looking at me like I kicked their favorite kid every time I take more meat than they get.

But it's not such a problem, as I have an easy solution for that.

Yup, it's Hadwin.

We're not hunting together anymore, obviously, but I still let him deal with social stuff. He seems to hate it, too, so that's a bonus.

It's not that easy to see, but I keep noticing his slow, annoyed blinking and veins on his neck every time he clenches his teeth.

I love it.

Screw you, Hadwin.

Now I'm going to hunt monsters or animals together with Tess and Kevin; sometimes, we also take some of the kids. Tess always makes sure that they know they might end up risking their lives, so that's it.

Sometimes they get hurt—a scratch here, a stab wound there—but Tess and Kevin make sure to cover for them. Especially Tess.

God damn.

She now walks around with, like, five spears somehow tied to her back, and she throws them while using her [Psychokinesis]. I'm sure at some point, she leveled up her skill, as they became much faster and more accurate. Combined with her [Farsight], it makes an amazing combination.

As for Kevin, he became a pretty reliable tank. His second skill, [Combustion], also helps, allowing him to cause objects or substances to ignite or even create controlled explosions.

Once again.

I'm not jealous, okay?

Also, I will have to find some really annoying work for Kevin.

Spoiled kids. Back in my day...

A few more days pass like this, and one more person dies; this time, it's Dominic.

For some time, he kept getting angrier and angrier, and the stares he gave Sophie and Hadwin were anything but friendly.

Then he disappeared.

No one saw anything.

No one knows anything.

But I have my own suspicions about what happened to the man.

Lily cried a little.

Sweet girl crying for a dead man she barely knew. The knowledge that he had passed away in a strange and distant land, so far from everyone he knew, only amplified her sorrow.

CHAPTER 31
SUNS GONE

The "suns" are gone once again. As before, a terrible wave of mana washes over the entire first floor before they disappear.

This time, it's a bit colder than before, so we collect more wood and hunt more animals, while expecting even colder weather next time. A few more people have learned how to skin them without damaging the skins, so we're keeping them in case another cycle becomes even colder. So we hunt as much as we can and smoke the meat.

There are more animals. There are more goblins, many more. And now, even groups of wolves have started attacking us.

In the forest around our camp, we've also found terribly mangled corpses of giant wolves and trolls.

We don't know for sure what monster did it, but I have my suspicion.

The Cinderbear.

Oh, I almost forgot.

Fuck that guy.

The corpses are mangled with limbs broken, torn-off limbs, and gouged-out inner organs, but they are not eaten, and that's what worries me the most.

Did the Cinderbear develop a taste for a human-based diet?

If yes, why hasn't he come back?

People would be terrified, so only a few of us know about mangled corpses.

The bus is even more "armored" now, and we're using bigger and bigger pieces of logs to make it more durable. It's still our go-to place to sleep or hide. Our surroundings have also changed a lot.

There is an insane number of sharpened logs pointing outward.

There are some palisades closer to the bus.

We are building pitfalls with more sharpened sticks inside them, and Hadwin has taught us to set up some traps.

We are also collecting as much food and water as we can.

And we are leveling up.

I don't even bother killing Level 2 monsters anymore; I just break their limbs and throw them in front of someone else to finish. Sure, it's less experience than if they killed it on their own, but it's something.

In all of this, I try to have some fun as well.

When I'm fighting anything under Level 5, I don't use any weapon, just my hands and mana.

It was a bit hard and awkward at the start, but now it has become good training for me. I've learned more about their physiology and weak points.

Oh, and the Level 7 troll we fought some time ago together with Tess and Kevin?

Well, it was a baby.

Just a cute little baby, and I think we found its mom. Or dad; who knows?

I'm sitting high up in a tree and looking down as the troll slowly comes closer and closer to where I am.

[Troll - Level 12]

During the past few days, I've been watching it together with Tess. From really far away, careful not to get noticed. We learned its routes, and the troll is more reliable than your country asking you for taxes. It always walks the same way, and we suspect it either comes from its *house* or goes toward it.

And now, we are here. We both washed in water, both our bodies and clothes, and then we threw some mud on ourselves and finished it by rubbing some plants onto our skin and clothes. All of this was to cover our smell as much as possible and to smell like the forest in hopes of avoiding its nose.

It truly has a humongous nose, I must say.

The troll's skin is more grayish this time, and it is probably fifty percent bigger than the baby we met. Its muscles look much more dangerous. The earth shakes a bit as it moves, and stones crack under its feet.

It moves closer and closer, and when it is right under me, Tess makes some noise where she is.

The monster instantly stops and looks toward her, smelling in that direction.

Nice timing.

Now it's up to me.

[Focus].

[Mana Manipulation].

I activate my skills, and my mind enters a calming, deeper state of focus. Everything other than this hunt ceases to matter.

I grip the mace and exhale.

The troll starts turning toward me when a spear comes flying out of nowhere and burrows deep into its left eye.

It roars, and another spear comes flying and shatters as it hits the troll's skin, unable to wound it at all.

The monster turns toward where the spears are flying from, and I jump down from the tree directly toward its head.

My muscles feel as if they are burning, and I swing my mace as hard as I can right at the back of the troll's head. The amount of mana going through my body is no joke, and I hear a crack as my mace hits the troll's head.

Crack.

Terrible wounds appear on the back of the troll's head, and the mace shatters to pieces. I throw away the now-useless handle, instantly pulling out the short sword I have with me.

The troll staggers, confused and most likely suffering from some brain damage.

Two more spears come flying and hit the troll's face, unable to do more than distract it.

I land on the troll's shoulders and dodge the hand reaching out for me.

[Oscillation].

I send mana through the handle of the sword and toward the blade. It creates a thin mana coating around one side of the blade.

My head hurts, and blood starts running from my nose.

I focus more and more.

Mana on the blade becomes denser and denser and moves toward the tip. Using the [Oscillation] skill, the blade begins to vibrate rapidly, its edges humming with energy. The swift back-and-forth motion of the mana enhances cutting power. With the full power of my mana-strengthened body, I stab the sword inside the wound left by the mace.

Then I hold on tightly to avoid falling and have to dodge its hands as the troll starts thrashing around. When given the opportunity, I pull out the sword and stab again right next to the first wound, but the blade bounces off the monster's head; [Oscillation] is gone, and even my [Focus] can't keep it running any longer.

So I stab the already existing wound again and again. Every time I do, the monster's roars become weaker and its movements slower.

A chilling, piercing noise fills the forest as the spear, propelled by [Psychokinesis], slices through the air like a deadly projectile. The steel blade gleams menacingly, streaking toward the troll's neck at breakneck speed. The terrifying combination of Tess's psychic force and the spear's sharpness drives it deep into the creature's flesh, leaving it lodged within its throat.

I stab again and move with the sword while it's lodged inside the troll's skull, squelching as I make a mess out of the monster's brain.

Finally, the troll starts falling to the ground, and while jumping down, I grab the spear and pull it out so it doesn't break.

You're welcome, Tess.

The monster lands, and I finally get the message.

> **[You have defeated a Troll - Level 12]**
> **[Level 8 > Level 9]**

I invest my stat points and look at Tess coming closer. She answers my unspoken question. "I did level up, yes."

Good.

The spears she threw float in the air, moving right toward her. She slowly checks them out, one after another, as they float around her in a circular orbit.

That's just showing off!

Well, whatever, just wait until my [Focus] shows its true power; even you will shudder in fear.

We get to the clearing, and I realize that we've been here a bit over a week. It's surprising to me how some people have adapted to all of this.

As more and more time passes and I observe them, I come to realize that none of us are normal.

Maybe it's not that we were randomly put into Hell Difficulty, but that we were put into Hell Difficulty because of who we are.

My theory is that the system places people into the difficulty it thinks is best for the person. As for the fact that an entire busload of people got here, maybe we are all suitable for Hell Difficulty?

There are so many people on Earth; there have to be groups of people together where all of them are a good fit for a specific difficulty, right?

Anyway, that's just a little theory I came up with.

What welcomes us at the clearing is an angry Hadwin stomping right toward us, a few people following him, probably wanting to enjoy the free show.

Well, I can't blame them. These days, it's hard to find something amusing to do.

CHAPTER 32
FIGHT WITH HADWIN

"**S**o you did it..."
You bet we wiped the floor with that Level 12 troll. No biggie.

Hadwin looks at me and Tess.

"Fucking hell, Nathaniel." He sighs and waves his hands around. "Do you have any idea how dumb that was?"

Dumb? Please! Only slightly dangerous.

"You could've fucking died!"

No worries! If it looked too dangerous, I'd run and bring him straight to our camp... Wait, what?

"I expected something like that from him, but even you, Tess?"

Huh? Should I feel insulted?

"You're putting all of our lives in danger, Nathaniel. Can you imagine how hard it would be if we lost both of you? Or if you didn't kill him and lured him back?"

Oh, so it's like that. It's not my problem, though.
Right, Tess?

I look at her, and she seems to be ashamed, just a tiny bit.

Lately, Hadwin has been more and more stressed as he deals with all of this. A lot of people just rely on him and let him lead them, and that puts a lot of pressure on him. Sophie creating her own group during all of that probably doesn't brighten his mood, either.

Well, that's something he decided to do, so suck it up.

As I try to pass by him, he steps in my way.

Uh?

Even people around us seem to be surprised and start whispering among themselves.

"Hadwin, I don't think it's a good idea..." Tess starts, but I filter out her voice and look at the man in front of me.

I look into his eyes, and he seems pretty serious.

So that's how it is. Feel free to try.

I enter [Focus] and then let a bit of my mana flow through my body.

Try it if you dare...

Then his fist hits me right in the face, and I stagger backward.

Huh?

Focus is gone, and so is the mana flowing through my veins.

He hits my face again, and I see blood. My blood.

What?

I try to collect mana and enter the [Focus], but I am unable to do so.

This time, he grabs my shoulders and strikes my stomach with his knee.

His kick is tough; air escapes my lungs, and a sharp, searing pain radiates through my abdomen. My muscles tense involuntarily, and for a moment, it feels as though

my insides are being crushed. Gasping for breath, I struggle to regain my composure.

I barely block his second kick and duck under his swing. His physical stats, like strength and dexterity, are higher, and without mana strengthening me, I am slower and weaker than him.

Slowly catching my breath and relaxing my mind, even without the skill, I continue to observe his movements.

I read his swing and block his fist with my hand. His hit sends me backward, and I use the moment to collect myself a bit more.

My face hurts, my stomach hurts, and I am unable to collect any mana.

Is it his skill?

I watch his movements, keeping my eyes on the center of his body—his shoulders, his legs, his waist.

I dodge another kick and swing. He is much quicker than me, so I have to start moving before he is halfway through his attack.

I counter in the middle of his attack, hitting his neck and forcing him backward. He makes a choking noise, and his hand goes up to cover his neck.

That gives me the opportunity to move closer and kick his knee. He staggers backward.

That's it?

I feint a hit at his neck with my fist. He moves his hand to block it, so I strike with my other hand.

That's all you can do?

I hit his stomach, and once more he staggers back. I kick his knee again. He grimaces from the pain. I take the moment to punch him in the eye.

I feel his skill deactivate, and I know that I can use my own skills again.

But I don't. Instead, I attack him with only the strength of my body.

I step closer and bury my knee into his stomach. He bends over, and I quickly hit the bottom of his chin.

He is faster, he is stronger, but his attacks are telegraphed and easy to dodge.

Another quick hit at his chin, and he staggers, feeling lightheaded as the hit shakes his brain inside his skull.

Two hits at his neck, and he makes a louder choking noise. I kick at his crotch; he tries to block it with his leg but is too shaken to do it in time.

As he falls to his knees, I twist my body, pull more strength into it, and give him as strong a punch as I can, right into the side of his face.

I stare at him as he lies there, unmoving. The others stare at him, too, and no one jumps in to help either of us.

After a while, he looks at me and weirdly smiles.

What's so funny, old man?

You got beaten, and I didn't even use mana, so what's so funny about that?!

WHAT IS SO FUNNY?!

"Hehe..." There is some blood on his teeth.

"You know it, too, right?" He laughs again. "I could have killed you if I really wanted to."

I remain silent.

"Hehe, you were ready for me, expecting an attack, but I still managed to land a few solid hits." He lies on the ground, gazing at the sky. "Wow, that was satisfying. I've wanted to smack you in the face for ages." He takes a moment. "You little punk."

My silence makes him laugh even more. "Finally, I can see some emotion on your face." He looks straight at

me. "You always look so uninterested, bored, even when fighting, but now...you look so angry."

I look around, and most of the people avoid my gaze. Lily and a few others are scared. Tess is standing close to me. Her face is hard to read, but she seems ready to move. Not to help me, just to stop me if I decide to finish off Hadwin.

"You know, lately, you've become too confident, Nathaniel, too fearless. You enjoy fighting too much; you risk a lot. Not only your life but also the lives of people around you." He looks straight into my eyes. "You are not undefeatable. You could have easily died today, and you can die from something else if you continue being so careless."

I look at Tess; she doesn't avoid my gaze but doesn't say anything, and that's enough for me.

I leave before I hurt someone. I enter the forest and slowly calm myself down.

Breathe in.

Breathe out.

Repeat.

I don't use [Focus]. I disable it as much as I can and think.

And think. And think more.

After calming down, I come to realize that both of us might be right. The truth is somewhere in the middle.

Sure, I can be more careful; actually, I need to be more careful and not blindly rely on my skills, as he showed me so *nicely*.

Damn that jerk.

On the other side, I can't just stop hunting and give up on becoming stronger. Sure, there is some risk, but something tells me that this first floor of Hell Difficulty is just the beginning. Taking it slowly and comfortably might not make me strong enough to survive the entire five years.

I will hunt, I will risk, I will enjoy the challenges, and I will continue using [Focus] to get rid of some useless emotions, as it's all for my survival.

As for Hadwin and his lesson? My thanks will be that I won't beat him senseless and will dial it down a bit. He is right about me being cocky.

So thank you, and fuck you.

As for which of us is right? Only time will tell.

CHAPTER 33
REVENGE

POV: KEVIN WILSON

It's the first time I've seen Nathaniel so angry; actually, it might be the first time I've seen him showing any strong emotion at all. He usually walks around looking like someone printed his resting face onto paper and then stuck it to his head.

Damn, for a second, I thought he might have killed Hadwin right here, right now.

I'm sure Tess would try to stop him, but I'm not sure if she would be able to if he really wanted to do it.

The scary part is that he didn't even use mana.

Like, what the hell, who does that?!

I didn't sense anything, but Kim told me that Hadwin did something to disrupt Nathaniel's mana. Then at some point during the fight, Nathaniel canceled the older man's skill, and even though he could use mana, he finished him off without even bothering to use it.

What a madlad. Again, who the hell does that?!

Right after the fight, he went into the forest. The way he just casually entered it while checking his surroundings sent shivers down my back. He's probably the only one who does that. The rest of us are still nervous every time we go hunting.

I get back to smoking boar meat and continue what I started before the fight happened.

"Do you think he's very angry?" Lily asks quietly.

"You saw his face; he's *suuuuper* pissed off."

"Oh..." She quiets down.

At this point, I am sure everyone can see that she's got a small crush on Nathaniel.

Well, probably everyone other than him. He doesn't seem to be too good with people stuff. He thinks he's careful, but I always notice how quickly he disappears every time more than one or two people talk to him. Sometimes he endures it a bit longer, but as time passes, he becomes quieter and quieter. Most of the time, it ends up with him just leaving or Tess saving him—or us?

It's kind of fun to mess with him a bit.

That isn't the main problem; the main problem is him being a selfish, mostly emotionless asshole.

But he's our selfish, mostly emotionless asshole.

I don't know if he's aware of it, but I'm sure that half of the people would already be dead if it wasn't for him; hell, probably even more.

Sure, he doesn't have to be such a dick about it.

I remember the time from a few days ago when he power-leveled Kim in exchange for his sword. Damn, he actually did take it without even a hint of hesitation after getting the boy to Level 4, leaving him unarmed.

He's ruthless, selfish, and somewhere in the back of my mind, I'm sure he doesn't care that much about any of us.

Yet...

He's always calm, and even when the levels of shit get deeper, he doesn't become desperate; he just listens, nods, and says one or two sentences, giving us something to do.

It's weirdly calming, having someone to rely on just a little bit.

Even while knowing how he feels about us.

When I return, the first to welcome me is the best doggo of the first floor of Hell Difficulty.

Yup, the shameless little bugger of a corgi is still alive and well, and I swear at this point, he might be heavier than some of the girls.

Goddamn, boy!

As I sit with my back against one of our palisades, he comes to me with something in his mouth.

A wallet.

What the hell?!

What the actual heck?!

Also, good boy. We'll split it 50/50.

I pet his head, which is still of a similar size to what it was at the start, and take the wallet from him while he swings his tail wildly. Once again, it looks like he's shaking his butt because of his short tail.

I open the wallet, and there's some cash, bank cards, one ID, and nothing more.

Hadwin Harper.

Oh my. It's getting better and better!

I quickly look around, but there are no witnesses... Uh, I mean, there's no one around.

I take all of the cash, probably around two hundred dollars, and close the wallet and give it back to the best boy.

"Can you put it back?"

He blinks slowly and runs back to where he came from.

Is this the first cash theft here? It must be, right?

Hehe.

Take that, old man!

I put the cash into my pocket and pull out the remaining pieces of the necklace that I got from the goblin shaman that I killed, which feels like weeks ago. It's still broken, and I only hold its pieces, but I keep coming back to it. I can feel some mana lingering on it, but I just can't find out what it's for and how it's etched into the pieces and able to stay there.

One good thing is that I improved my usage of [Oscillation] thanks to studying the necklace, so that's something.

Biscuit comes back and lies on the ground next to me, putting his head on my thigh. He closes his eyes.

At this point, I'm almost sure that he's the smartest one out of all of us here. He knows how to behave around me and never becomes too annoying. And then there are things like Hadwin's wallet.

It's weird, but I think he saw us fighting and wanted to help me get some petty revenge and get into my good graces.

I'm not crazy! That must be it.

I slowly pat his small head and enter a bit deeper into [Focus] to start training my [Mana Manipulation]. After a while, Tess comes to me.

"Hey..." she starts carefully.

"It's okay." I only say that much, but she will understand.

I know she partly agrees with Hadwin, but she wasn't able to tell that to me for some reason. Hell, I probably wouldn't even listen, so I can't actually be mad at her for not helping me or being ready to try to stop me if I tried to do something worse to Hadwin.

After a while, she gives one of her tiny smiles and sits next to me. She pokes Biscuit's bulging belly, and the dog

opens one of his eyes and then closes it when he sees it's Tess. That makes her poke him a few more times, but the good boy ignores her, so she stops.

Corgi 1, human 0.

"Kim got his [Telekinesis] to Level 3, and Lily got [Rejuvenation] to Level 2," she informs me.

Damn, what is that scrawny boy eating and doing? Level 3 already?

"She can heal small and slightly bigger scratches now, but still only her own. She wasn't able to heal others."

Oh, that's a shame, but no worries, we will get there. My personal healing station is coming along nicely.

Tess doesn't continue, so I guess others weren't able to level up any skills. The annoying thing is that I don't know if the speed at which we are leveling up our skills is good or bad. There is nothing to compare it to, just us.

Out of nowhere, I get an idea.

"Hey, Tess?"

"Hm?" She leans a bit closer, and I put my hand into my pocket and pull out a one-hundred-dollar bill, a gift from one unnamed guy.

"Can you go and buy me some sweets?" I hand her the banknote.

She looks at me, then at the bill.

Back at me and then once again at the bill.

Her confused face is so funny.

"Did you steal it from Hadwin?" she instantly guesses outright.

Crap, am I that predictable?

Oh, wait a moment! I didn't do it; I almost forgot.

I point at the sleeping corgi, and she rolls her eyes.

"Sure." She just stands up and leaves.

The banknote stays behind.

Two hours later, the Cinderbear appears again.

CHAPTER 34
WEAK

The once-peaceful forest transforms into an eerie, unsettling place. Every rustle and crack makes my heart race, and the sense of foreboding grows heavier with each passing second.

It is then that the monster makes its entrance. Emerging from the dense foliage, the giant gray bear steps into the clearing with a deliberate, unhurried pace.

The bear's enormous paws make a sickening crunch as they crush the underbrush and fallen leaves. Its massive size and power are evident in the way the ground trembles with each step it takes.

The most chilling aspect of the giant gray bear's appearance, however, is its eyes.

They glow with an unnatural orange light, as if fueled by a fire that burns within the monster itself.

A wave of mana hits the clearing, and everyone becomes paralyzed with fear.

As the bear continues its slow, methodical advance, the forest grows quieter and quieter.

Its low growl reverberates through the air, a rumbling sound that makes your body shake.

Once again, the bear looks at me and then at the ground in front of it.

[Cinderbear - Level 20]

The creature has leveled up.

Waves of mana I feel from the bear make my stomach clench, and my entire body feels as if it isn't getting enough air. It is even hard to breathe.

The bear takes a few steps toward us and then stops, looking at us with its wild but intelligent eyes. Someone screams out of fear and desperation. Its ears perk up, and it growls. I flinch and try to run, but my body refuses to. I'm paralyzed and can only stand there and look around. The others seem to be in a similar state. The monster roars loud enough to shatter the remaining windows and threaten to burst my eardrums.

"What does it want?!"

"I-I can't run."

"Can we fight it?"

"He should fight it!"

"Maybe it's friendly?"

Then someone says something I've been thinking about:

"Maybe it wants to eat something? Just like last time?"

Everyone falls silent, and we all remember the scene of Damon's body being slowly consumed by the bear. The monster growls and moves even closer. As it walks, it steps on a few spikes and hits several palisades with its paw. The pieces of wood shatter without dealing any damage.

With the memory of Damon's gruesome fate fresh in our minds, people exchange scared glances, unsure of how to handle the terrifying beast. The bear is getting closer and closer, and the fear is becoming worse and worse.

Our feet feel glued to the ground.

The air feels thicker now, and cold sweat is running down my back.

I thought I might be able to do something the next time we met the bear, but no, I can't do anything. Even thinking about running away feels impossible.

I feel...pathetic.

In a moment of selfish desperation, Ethan screams, his face twisted with panic. "Maybe we can throw it someone, just like last time! We should give it...someone."

His eyes dart around, searching for the weakest among us, hoping to save himself at the expense of another. The group recoils in horror at the suggestion, but the fear makes it hard to dismiss his idea completely.

Ethan's eyes land on Sophie's sister, but he quickly changes his mind, and his eyes stop at Lily, a petite, defenseless-looking girl. "We should... I'm sorry..." He desperately moves closer and grabs her; she screams.

At the moment, no one is able to move, so they react a bit late as he instantly starts pulling her closer to throw her at the bear.

I agree with him. He is most likely right. He is only trying to save his life.

But...

What does he think he is doing?

In front of me?!

I'm finally able to take a step and grab his neck while strengthening myself with mana. I break the hand he put

on Lily, and he screams in pain. Then I pull him away from the girl, toward the bear.

I am thankful, Ethan, you made the first move; at this moment, you were more decisive than me.

But...

That girl is someone I know a bit. I've talked with her a little, and she always tries to speak nicely to me and not annoy me. You, on the other hand, I don't know. You're a stranger to me.

So it's not a hard decision.

I pull him away from the others and throw him toward the bear while strengthening my body. He flies through the air, hits the ground, and then rolls until he stops right in front of the bear.

He looks up, shaken and confused, and screams upon seeing the bear's maw right in front of him.

He uses his skill, and a light blue, thin barrier of mana appears around him.

Meanwhile, my eyes meet those of the Cinderbear, and I feel a wave of mana from it, while it ignores the screaming human beneath it. Then it turns its attention back to Ethan.

The barrier instantly breaks the moment the monster touches it with its paw.

Crack.

It steps onto Ethan's left hand. The shield made of mana flashes into existence once more but instantly breaks. The bear bites his other hand, pulling it off with a wet sound of tearing muscles and tendons.

Ethan is still screaming.

He's still alive as the Cinderbear slowly chews his hand while curiously looking down at the man.

Then the bear leans closer and takes a bite of the man's belly.

I'll remember his screams until the day I die.

Slowly, they become weaker and weaker; he coughs up a lot of blood and then passes out.

The monster slowly eats the entire man while casually glancing around, looking at us.

There isn't even a hint of wariness toward us as it finishes its meal.

After it's done, it licks its maw, and another pulse of mana flashes toward me. This time, I am able to sense that it's focused on the broken necklace in my pocket.

Then the Cinderbear leaves once more.

A few hours after the bear leaves, I go into the forest. Alone.

I hunt and kill everything I can find. Trolls, goblins, wolves, animals. I murder anything I see. Rage and mana are burning in my veins as I do so.

I've never felt so weak.

I've never felt so defenseless.

All I could do was watch and sit there, not even able to run. Just helplessly wait and hope one man would be enough.

Pathetic.

I hate it, I despise it, I don't want to feel like this.

Never again.

Time passes, and I finally get the message I want.

[You have defeated a Troll – Level 11]
[Level 9 > Level 10]
Well done! The Side Quest has been
successfully completed. Please select one of
the traits. The traits are based on your actions
and performance up until now within the
Tutorial.

Be advised: humans are limited to three traits.
Choose with caution.

The system has become nicer.

CHAPTER 35
TRAITS

When I come back bloodied and tired but satisfied, I find everyone packing. Some are collecting food and hides, while others are making sure we will take enough water to last us for a while by gathering all useful stuff.

The decision is unanimous.

Rather than waiting for the Cinderbear to appear once again, everyone prefers just moving somewhere else in hopes it won't find us.

I agree, even though I am unhappy about that. It's a smart decision, but it still feels sour, as if I am leaving behind unsolved problems. The Cinderbear is terrifying, but I want revenge before the first floor ends.

"Tess, can you keep a watch over me for a few minutes?" I instantly find the girl by her mana signature.

Hearing something in my voice, she doesn't ask where I went and what I want and just nods solemnly.

I enter the bus and move to the last seat, the seat I sat in when we got here.

I breathe in. Let's see.

"Trait," I say.

Please select one of the traits that are based on your actions and performance up until now within the Tutorial.

Be advised: humans are limited to three traits. Available traits:

Enhanced Mana Heart (Passive)
Augments the user's natural mana pool and regeneration rate, allowing for longer and more sustained use of mana-based abilities. This passive trait enables the user to cast more spells and maintain their magical abilities with less downtime, providing a significant advantage in extended battles and outside of them.

Regenerative Tissue (Passive)
The user's body gains the ability to regenerate tissue rapidly, accelerating the healing of wounds and reducing the impact of injuries during combat. This trait not only helps the user recover from injuries more quickly but also ensures that they remain in peak fighting condition, even in the most grueling of encounters.

Mana Circuit (Passive)
Integrates a network of mana channels throughout the user's body, optimizing the distribution of mana and amplifying the power of their mana-based abilities without additional mana consumption. This enhancement allows the user to draw upon their mana more efficiently, resulting in more potent spells and abilities while reducing overall mana expenditure.

Adaptive Resistance (Passive)
Temporarily and gradually adjusts the user's resistances based on the types of damage they receive, allowing them to become more resilient against recurring threats over time. As the user encounters different forms of attack, their body learns to adapt and develop natural defenses against those specific damage types, providing a growing advantage in combat.

Mana-Infused Vitality (Passive)
Considerably strengthens the constitution by allowing the user's mana to bolster their natural vitality, resulting in a drastic improvement in overall health, stamina, and recovery rate. This infusion of mana into the user's body grants them increased durability and resilience, allowing them to endure more punishment and recover more quickly from damage.

Mana Sensitive Skeleton (Passive)
The user's bones become highly sensitive to mana, allowing them to channel and store mana within their skeletal structure. Additionally, this heightened sensitivity enables the user to better detect and sense mana within their own body and the surrounding environment, increasing their awareness of magical presences and activities.

Efficient Mana Conversion (Passive)
Increases the user's proficiency in converting their mana into different forms of energy, such as thermal, kinetic, or electrical, granting them a wider range of abilities and techniques in combat. This mastery over mana conversion allows the user to adapt their abilities to suit the situation at hand, providing a versatile and unpredictable fighting style.

Spell Diffusion (Passive)
This trait allows the user to diffuse a portion of incoming magical attacks, scattering the energy and reducing the overall impact on the user. This ability is especially useful in battles against magic-wielding foes, as it weakens their power and provides a defensive advantage to the user.

Reinforced Musculature (Passive)
Strengthens the user's muscles with an infusion of mana, granting them increased physical power and the ability to perform feats of strength beyond their natural capabilities. This trait not only enhances the user's offensive capabilities but also allows them to perform impressive physical feats that may be useful outside of combat.

Kinetic Channeling (Passive)
Enables the user to channel their mana into kinetic energy, allowing them to enhance their physical movements and attacks. This trait provides the user with the ability to perform faster, more agile, and more powerful physical actions, making them a formidable force in close-quarters combat.

Wow, that's a lot.

I expected a few traits, and here we go, ten of them and even with descriptions!

What the hell? Who are you, and what did you do to the system we all knew and hated?

I'm not complaining, just curious.

Also, any new skills for me? You know, I find it unfair as some people started with diamond spoons in their mouths.

Just look at Tess! At this point, the stones she throws with her [Psychokinesis] feel more dangerous than bullets, and Sophie is walking through the forest while manipulating monsters so they are unable to see her until she stabs her spear up their rear ends.

Look, I'm not ungrateful, but maybe, maybe, one OP skill? Just one.

...

Yeah, I thought so. Screw you, too! It's not like I wanted something from you or anything, stupid!

Now, back to traits. They look amazing, all of them. Unfortunately, I can pick only one, but in the future, there will probably be more opportunities, as it's said humans can have three of them.

Does that mean that there are different beings than humans that can get more or fewer traits?

Probably? But that's a problem for tomorrow me.

For a start, I read over them a few more times and try to think of all the usages and which trait could be the best, not only for immediate growth but also to aid my growth in the future.

Enhanced Mana Heart (Passive). One mystery is solved. The thing that gives all of us mana, regenerates it, and collects it is called Mana Heart. It's either somewhere within my current heart or it replaces my heart with a new one. Either way, I like this one, and it seems like a strengthened version of it.

Regenerative Tissue (Passive). This one sounds really good, too, as it would help me to heal from wounds faster than just increasing my constitution. But still, I like the first option more.

Mana Circuit (Passive). This is a serious contender for the first spot. Darn, I already know that I will have a hard time deciding which one to pick.

Adaptive Resistance (Passive). This one is meh. Sure, it sounds good, but I'd rather have something that will allow me to end the fight faster.

Mana-Infused Vitality (Passive). Similar to Regenerative Tissue.

Mana Sensitive Skeleton (Passive). Something I got thanks to my [Mana Perception]? Not bad, but I still like Circuit and Mana Heart more.

Efficient Mana Conversion (Passive). Sounds interesting, but it's a trap! I'm sure I can learn to convert mana into different forms on my own, and now I even have hints. Hahaha. So thermal, kinetic, electrical, and probably much more. But let's start experimenting with these three.

Spell Diffusion (Passive). Good, but I need something more versatile and something that can increase my damage.

Reinforced Musculature (Passive). This one is probably from the continuous strengthening of my body.

Kinetic Channeling (Passive). This one is also a no.

So that's it. It's either Enhanced Mana Heart or Mana Circuit.

Which one should I pick?

CHAPTER 36
TRAIT ACQUIRED

In the end, I pick the trait, and the window disappears.

> **Congratulations! You have acquired Mana Circuit (passive)**
> **Trait 1/3**

I immediately feel my heartbeat race, and warmth washes over my body. My heart goes into overdrive and sends wave after wave of mana through my body. At first, it's only warm, but quickly, it feels as if someone set a red-hot wire through my body. I clench my teeth, but I quietly groan.

Forget anything nice I said about the system.

The pain becomes stronger and stronger as the system etches a network of mana channels through my body. Mana travels from my heart toward the tips of my fingers, up my skull, everywhere, leaving a burning sensation in its wake.

After what feels like an hour, the pain slowly subsides and is replaced by a feeling of lightheadedness, as if I'm about to pass out.

Damn, I can't wait to go through this two more times!

Someone, please, send help.

Ha, whatever.

Still lightheaded, I send mana through my body and stop instantly.

Ehm?

I try again.

And again.

What the heck?!

I take back everything I said. Give me more! More pain, more circuits!

It feels as if, up until now, I kept using a fork to eat soup, but then someone bonked the back of my head and put a spoon in my hand.

It feels so much more natural to take mana from my Mana Heart and use it.

Also, the network of mana etched into me feels as if someone replaced an old road with a high-speed highway.

What the heck!

I almost want to forgive the system for playing favorites, but at this point, I'm sure that the traits others will get will be better than mine.

But that won't be able to quiet down my happiness.

I move mana all over my body; it's so fluid, so quick, and the amount I can move is much finer and more accurate than before. Now instead of using a river of mana, I can send a thin thread of mana through my circuit for more delicate control.

It's as if I used too much mana before because of my terrible body and low mana conductivity.

But dang, it just shows how unprepared and inefficient the human body is for handling mana.

> [Mana Manipulation - Level 5 > Mana Manipulation - Level 6]

Here we go!

I get on my feet, and as I walk, my body still screams, but now I am more content with the pain.

"Finally!" Kevin sounds super annoying. Even more so now when my head is still hurting.

But I'll let it go, just this time! Because I'm in a good mood.

"Even Burrito is ready to go."

Okay, he's not making it easy.

He laughs. "Also, you walk like you crapped yourself."

Well, that's it.

"Hey, hey, Nat. Why are you looking at me like that?"

Hmm, maybe I should make him skin more deer? I think he really disliked it a lot.

"Nat? Nathaniel, stop, wait a bit."

Biscuit greets me by wagging his tail and continues walking next to me.

"Look, it was just a joke. You know that, right? Just a joke, I didn't even mean it. You know how I am, right? Hehe."

I might make him train his skill a bit more. I'll help, obviously! I can throw some stones at him to reflect.

Maybe I can use a bit more mana this time; it will help him improve faster.

"Nathaniel...? Sir?"

He stops somewhere behind me, and I join Tess and Hadwin.

The girl greets me, but Hadwin only nods. He's trying not to show it, but I see the corners of his lips lifting up just a tiny bit.

Dang, are you remembering punching my face, old man?

Tess starts talking. "You seem to be ready, so we can leave in a few minutes. As we decided in the talk before, you and I will be scouts, and Sophie, Kevin, and Kim will move a bit further behind us, followed by Hadwin and the others."

"What about the dog? He seems to be uncooperative lately..." The look he gives to Biscuit doesn't seem that friendly. Not at all.

What the heck did you do to him, Biscuit?

Good boy!

We are all looking down at him, and the best corgi sticks out his tongue while breathing. He looks so cheeky, he's almost smiling.

The dog looks at me, and I look at him; for a few seconds, our gazes meet.

"Stay with Hadwin and the others," I say.

His tail stops swinging from side to side, and he slowly blinks.

"So we walk until it's about time for the night to come?" I ask.

"Wait, that's it for Burrito? Did he understand or something?" Kevin says something in the background, but most of us have already learned to mostly ignore him.

Someone already calculated the time when the suns are going to disappear by looking at the system countdown until forced return, and now we can predict it pretty accurately.

"We can walk for like five to seven hours, and after that, we will have to set up somewhere and build at least some defense. A few hours should be enough."

It's all the things we talked about before, so I start to filter them out and continue focusing on training my [Mana Manipulation]. The good thing is that my [Oscillation] has become easier to use, and now I can keep it up longer.

I glance down at my finger and the blade of mana created around it. When I activate the [Oscillation], the difficulty goes up pretty fast, but it's doable so far.

The blade of mana oscillates wildly, and I keep it up for as long as I can before it slips out of my control and dissolves.

New record!

Just a bit more, and I might be able to coat the entire blade of my short sword with it.

Then Tess pokes my shoulder, and I look up. Everyone is staring at me.

Did I miss something?

Hadwin sighs.

Why do you sound so annoyed? I just practiced a little bit! You don't have to be such a jerk about it!

Biscuit, defend me!

I look down, and the doggo is already jumping around a butterfly.

" ... "

He catches it and eats it. Then he spits it out. He looks at me, sticking out his tongue, trying to get rid of the taste.

Biscuit...

God bless your poor soul.

Tess and I enter the forest first. Even though I am walking ahead of her, Tess is the one pointing where we should go, as her skill somehow allows her to see through the dense forest. *Why not call it X-ray vision? Why Farsight? Huh? System?*

There is no answer, and we continue scouting ahead of the others while Tess seamlessly points me in the right direction.

You know, we came up with a code.

I have my [Mana Perception] activated, and when I feel her collecting the mana in her right hand, I go right; the same goes for left. If she collects mana in her chest, that means there is a monster. If she collects it in both of her legs, there is a strong monster, and we have to run. Stuff like that.

To be honest, our cooperation has become pretty good lately, and we can quietly go through the forest while leaving marks for the others.

Sometimes we kill one or two monsters, but that's it; the forest is quiet.

The wind blows gently, moving the leaves and creating shifting shadows on the ground. Sunlight streams through the branches, making the forest look lively and bright. The sun feels warm on my skin, the breeze is cool and refreshing, and the forest has a pleasant smell.

"Such a pretty day..." Her voice is soft and quiet, and I slow down to end up walking next to her, loosening some tension from my body.

If she doesn't see any monster, there's no way I will, even with my [Mana Perception] active.

"Yes."

I look up at the sky, and the wind messes with my hair a bit. As I walk through the woods, I notice how the trees

seem to create a natural rhythm with the swaying of their branches. The forest is quiet, devoid of the typical sounds of animals and birds, adding to the sense of solitude. The fresh air fills my lungs as I take a deep breath, and I can't help but feel a sense of calm and stillness.

Out of nowhere, Tess laughs quietly while covering her mouth with a hand.

"I'm sorry, but I just remembered the poor deer you tried to skin before. Nothing against your skills, of course."

Whoa, such a low blow.

"Don't look at me like that," she whispers and smiles at me. It's the first real smile I've seen on her face since we entered the first floor. "It's not like I'm lying."

Maybe you are not, but please be a bit less happy about that. You will bring Bambi's curse on us.

We continue walking in silence.

CHAPTER 37
NEW HOME

"**N**o, no. You have to use much less mana. Right now, you're wasting a lot of it. Also, try doing it a bit faster."

"It's not that easy!" Tess furrows her brow.

I continue to bully Tess while teaching her to improve her [Mana Manipulation]. With my trait, my handling of mana has improved a lot, and I don't feel that bad about her getting such good skills.

I'm helping her, right? I'm totally not doing it because of some petty reason, like her laughing at me and surely summoning a poor dead deer curse on us—Bambi's curse.

Not at all!

"Faster!"

Oh, Tess! Don't look at me like that! It's for your own good.

She sighs. "There's a troll in front of us. This way."

She points toward her right, and with a short nod, I head there while pulling out my sword. Soon enough, I see a baby troll.

> ### [Troll - Level 6]

Right now, I'm at a higher level than the monster, but I'm sure that it's still much stronger than me, and its constitution is higher.

As many times before, a rain of small stones flies like bullets from Tess into the troll's face. They hit it hard. Most of them shatter on its skin, but some hit its weaker points, such as its eyes.

The troll roars and turns to me, sniffing. It covers its eyes and swings its hand at me.

This time, I send a pulse of my mana toward the bottom half of my body and dash to the side. The troll is too slow to react, and my sword's blade passes through its legs like they're made out of butter. The blade, coated in oscillating mana, cuts through it like that.

With another roar full of pain, the creature loses its balance and falls down. I dodge slightly, making a diagonal cut across its face, deep enough to split it open. I move just in time to avoid a shower of its brain matter and blood.

> ### [You have defeated a Troll - Level 6]

"There are fewer and fewer goblins and more trolls; do you think we entered their territory or something?"

"It looks like it. We can be thankful that we ended up surrounded by goblins and not trolls."

"Just one troll would be enough to tear through us..."

Yup, exactly.

That's what I've been saying the entire time. After seeing the monsters that are lurking around, I know that we were super lucky.

Or maybe not?

Maybe the system put us in a slightly less dangerous starting zone?

We continue.

"So you were saying that I should get Mana Circuit as a trait if it's offered to me?"

"Probably? You might get offered something better, but right now, I think picking it was the right decision."

"No, I think you're right. Humans probably don't have bodies evolved to handle mana, so giving it a push like that sounds logical."

Right? I think so, too!

"But Mana Heart also sounded good."

Hmm, how to explain it?

"Imagine that you have a car."

I move under a few branches and hold one up so Tess can walk under it as well. Then I wait for her to finish leaving the mark on the tree.

"You collect enough money, and you buy a bigger engine. A much bigger engine goes into the car, and the rest of the car remains the same. At some point, you go out, excited to try it..."

"Oh, but then you step on the gas, the car rushes ahead, and it breaks?"

"It either breaks, or you won't be able to handle it. You can't turn the wheel easily anymore, because it's so much stronger. You can't stop quite as fast, because it's so much heavier."

She falls deep into her thoughts.

"I think I agree with you somewhat."

I see that I still haven't persuaded her completely, but that's okay.

But let's not tell her that I am doing the exact opposite with my stats.

Yup, do as I say, not as I do! What I'm doing could surely be considered dumb.

She should decide for herself and then bear the consequences or fruits of her decision.

"Let's wait for the second group and exchange information."

I only nod, and we wait in silence while keeping a watch.

After five or so minutes, I feel a wave of mana wash over my body. When it senses my mana signature, it instantly pulls back. After a minute or so, Sophie, Kevin, and Kim appear from the forest.

"Hello, fellow scouts." Kevin smiles brightly, and I sigh, already getting tired.

I let Tess deal with them, and for a second, my eyes meet those of a thin Korean boy wearing big glasses.

He smiles awkwardly and shrugs his shoulders, then looks away.

My best test subj— my best student!

Other than mine, his [Mana Manipulation] is the highest level, and his skill... [Telekinesis] seems to be a bit weaker version of Tess's [Psychokinesis], as I think Tess can do much more than just manipulate objects with her mind. Also, the raw power of her skill seems to be stronger than Kim's.

But the boy got another skill, [Gravity Well]. It's still low level, but as for now, he can increase or decrease the weight of items he's touching, but in the future...

Okay, breathe in, breathe out.

Good.

Now don't whine; it's getting annoying.

Good.

The power of self-reflection!

Anyway, he is an extremely hard-working and smart boy, but the weirdest thing is that he seems to be the happiest to be here out of all the kids.

Yes, even more than Kevin.

He's not showing it that much, but I can feel it in the way he manipulates his mana with excitement. I often see him looking around while smiling gently and just taking in the air.

Well, as I said some time ago, we might all be weirdos, and that's why we ended up here.

They talk for a bit longer and then leave. As they are going, I can feel Sophie looking for targets for her [Manipulation] and using it as detection. It's pretty shrewd.

"We have two more hours, and then we will have to set up camp and set up some defenses," Tess says.

Seems doable enough.

Behold!

My nature-inspired abode with a classic touch. Constructed from stones sourced from the earth's depths. It's cool and pleasant, ensuring a comfortable summer climate.

Spacious enough to accommodate around twenty guests!

The entrance is...

Yes, yes...it's a cave.

For heaven's sake.

It's wet, it's cold, it smells, and I really hope it isn't a place where the Cinderbear likes to take a nap.

After looking around for, like, thirty minutes, we don't find anything, so we decide to set up our camp here.

Everyone else already joined us, and plenty of people with superhuman strength start cutting down the trees, moving giant stones to create a wall, and trying to make this dump...our camp as comfortable as possible.

Somehow Kevin ended up having to help move the heaviest stones.

Damn.

How could that happen?

Please, don't look at me like that while moving that stone; people will think you hate me!

Well, as the strongest, I keep watch with Sophie...

Someone, *Hadwin*, did recommend Tess to use her psychokinesis to move heavy stuff, so I ended up keeping watch with Ms. Mindbender.

At some point, her pulses of mana become really annoying.

Not because of frequency but because of how they feel. It's as if someone keeps randomly lowering and increasing the volume on a song playing through a speaker.

I restrain myself, not wanting to help her at all, but after about thirty minutes, it becomes even more annoying. *How are you not improving?*

More time passes, and I swear she is even worse than before. At some point, she tried to experiment a bit, and it somehow made it even more annoying.

Oh, come on.

"Hey..." She turns to me, not even expecting me to talk to her. "Don't move your mana like this. Try..."

I continue to give her small tips on how to better handle her mana. Not too much, just a tiny piece of advice to make her probing less annoying.

The way she does it feels like looking for someone while screaming right next to their ear and asking where they are.

She listens quietly and tries it a few times, and I continue to correct her every time she does it wrong. I do it like twenty times, but she still continues and tries to fix it without complaining.

Her last try feels much better than what she's been doing the entire time, so I stop and leave her to her own practice.

She's a bit better now, and I breathe with satisfaction. It really annoyed me.

Both of us keep watch like this for the remainder of the time—until a sweaty and breathless Kevin comes to us.

"Damn, can't you two sit further from each other? A bit more, and you won't be able to see each other." He giggles; even tired, he has enough energy for his nonsense.

"Dinner's ready. Tess should be here soon to take over watching."

Seeing no reaction, the boy leaves, and I continue to watch while feeling the pulses of Sophie's mana near me.

Only then do I realize who I helped, and uncertainty washes over me.

Did I really do it just because I got annoyed? I didn't feel her mana touching my body, and I kept [Focus] running the entire time.

Still, I'm unsure if I'll ever be certain about her manipulating me or not.

CHAPTER 38
"MEOW"

After dinner, I take Kim, Lily, and Kevin to the side and continue to teach them a bit. We still have around one hour until the sun disappears, so why not spend it trying to learn something new in the way they use their skills?

I already nearly gave up trying to learn Lily's two starting skills. I really want her [Rejuvenation], as it sounds super useful, but even she can't use it that well, which makes it even harder. Her other skill, well, it sounds terrifying: [Disintegration]. She wasn't even able to activate it, so we can only guess what it does. But judging from the name... Damn, it sounds scary.

I keep my [Focus] up and running as well as my [Mana Perception] and continue to watch Kim move stones with his mind and mana, and throw them at Kevin, who reflects them back at the younger boy. Kim catches them with his skill, and the cycle repeats.

I wish they would go a bit harder. Reflecting it with more strength or using telekinesis with a bit more power to get more from Kevin. But they are holding back a little.

Obviously, they don't hold back when they are practicing with me. They use so much power that it looks like they are fighting for their lives.

That's because of my excellent teaching skills!

Old school ways, if you know what I mean.

I am resting against the wall inside the cave, and Lily is sitting near me, both of us watching the boys practice. While doing so, Lily keeps making tiny cuts with my knife into her arm and then healing them with her skill.

Once again, I wish she would cut more deeply, but that might be my dimmed feelings talking. Cutting yourself with ease isn't something people usually do.

"You remind me of my cat," Lily says quietly out of nowhere. Quiet enough so only I can hear her.

Huh? Is she dissing me?

There is a smile on her face when I turn to her.

"The way you quietly watch everything around you with curious eyes," she says, and her smile becomes a bit more longing.

Thank you?

"Grumpy also likes to just sit there and watch people, but he becomes really annoyed when someone tries to pet him. Most of the time, he just ignores people as they try to be friendly with him." She quietly laughs. "He just ignores it, but sometimes he gets his little acts of revenge. Once, I found a dead mouse in my bed after I kept making him try on some cat clothes."

Damn, I think I would like Grumpy a lot.

"But once in a while, he likes to come to people he trusts and snuggle with them, to share some warmth and spend

time together." Her big eyes look at me. "But only for a while. After just a moment, he leaves and is on his own."

Her face is so serious, as if she's talking to me about the truths of the universe.

But somehow, I don't mind it that much.

Not knowing why, I just open my mouth slightly and let out a very quiet sound.

"*Meow.*"

Her face is amazing to look at.

From pure shock to confusion, and then a giant smile appears on her face, quickly followed by a loud laugh.

She's laughing even as Kim and Kevin turn to her; she's laughing like she really needed to do so.

The darkness comes once again. As always, right after the change, the monsters and animals become much more aggressive.

Kevin charges up the stone with his [Combustion] and throws it at the troll. The stone flies through the air, emitting heat and shining in a bright orange color. Soon enough, it explodes, and the monster staggers back, covering its face with one hand.

Tess's spear flying through the air makes a terrifying whistling sound as it lands in the troll's belly with such brutal force, it nearly exits out the other side.

ROAR.

It seems to be going pretty well, so I ignore the rest of the fight and turn to look at my opponent.

Well, well, well, if it isn't the well-known small green jerk.

> **[Goblin Warrior – Level 5]**

He is slightly wounded. We spotted a fight between a group of goblins and a lone troll, so obviously, we decided to interrupt it.

I dodge to the side and quickly kick at the goblin. To my surprise, the green monster blocks it with the palm of his hand, leaving deep scratches on my shin.

Right after, he rushes at me with his mouth wide open. I dart to the side, but he throws a knife at me and then, with amazing speed, dashes at me on all fours, pumping his arms to move faster.

Instead of weaving, I deflect the knife with my sword and swing it at the goblin, who ducks right under it.

What the hell, is he some martial arts master?

I hit him with my knee, but he blocks it. The force of my kick sends him reeling, and he's able to leave more scratches on me, this time around my knee.

Okay, this is getting ridiculous.

I let mana flow through my body, and I dash at the same time he does. He also pulls out another knife, this one a bit shorter than the previous one.

This time, I grab his forearm, and while strengthening my body, I turn around and throw him against a tree. He hits it with a loud crack. Before he gets a chance to catch his breath, I attack him once more, slashing with my sword.

Unbelievably, he ducks by letting himself fall on his backside.

But this time, I expect it, and my left knee hits the side of his head. As he's trying to get up from the ground, I stab my blade through his chest.

[You have defeated a Goblin Warrior - Level 5]

Maybe I should invest some points into my dexterity and strength. It's pretty hard to deal with opponents like this without using mana to strengthen myself.

Or should I continue this way and invest most of my points into mana and constitution? Up until now, I did that with this logic—the more mana, the better. I can use it to strengthen myself and my other skills, too. In the future, I will get more of them, so a huge mana pool would be amazing.

And the stats I used for constitution helped me get a stronger body, able to handle wounds even without a healing skill, and strong enough to handle the mana.

But damn, it's kind of annoying seeing how troublesome it is to deal with a slightly skilled opponent when I'm not using mana.

I'll have to rethink it later.

When I turn back to the group, the troll and the remaining normal goblins are already dead, so they take all of the useful weapons and move back while Tess and I continue deeper into the forest.

Our goal this time is to get Tess to Level 10. She should be fairly close, so we look for more opponents to defeat.

I feel a pulse of mana from her right hand, quickly followed by a pulse from her chest and then a weaker one from both of her legs.

To my right, enemy, strong, maybe run? I translate it as such and continue toward my right.

Tess is sometimes a bit too careful for my taste, so it's up to me to push and put us in some danger with hopefully good rewards.

What we find is a massive, white-furred wolf. Its eyes are red and look right at us.

Somehow, it looks almost bored.

[Crimsonwolf - Level 12]

This time, I don't hold back and let mana flow through my circuit, strengthening my entire body.

[Focus] makes colors less vibrant, and the sounds of the wind, leaves, and trees cracking disappear somewhere into the back of my head.

Breathe in, breathe out.

I point toward the ground with three of my fingers and rush at the wolf. I run straight at him while Tess stays behind me, ready.

One second.

The wolf still seems to be bored and only turns to me; there is an almost curious look on its face.

Two seconds.

It changes its stance and shows us its teeth. Its eyes instantly go from curious to dangerous, and a wave of mana hits my body, slightly slowing me down. To counter it, I let more mana flow through my circuit and continue shortening the distance.

Three seconds.

I feint to the side, and immediately, Tess's spear hurtles through the air with terrifying speed, its flight enhanced by her skill. As it slices through the air, it emits a spine-chilling, pitched sound.

The wolf easily evades it.

Damn.

A wave of mana sends me flying backward against a tree. The air escapes my chest, and I let go of the sword in my hand.

When I look up, the wolf is still standing there.

The massive, majestic-looking white wolf stands out even more in the darkness, lit only by pink, green, and blue aurora-like lights. Mana pulses from the wolf's body flow into the surroundings, making smaller trees and branches bend and lean away from it. Its eyes look at us with something I can't explain as anything other than amusement.

The red eyes seem to be burning with an inner fire.

I feel the wolf's mana move.

Not good.

I stop focusing on efficiency and let the entirety of my mana roar through my body as I run.

The ground around the wolf shakes as it uses the same skill it used to attack me to propel itself forward with an insane boost.

This time, its target is Tess.

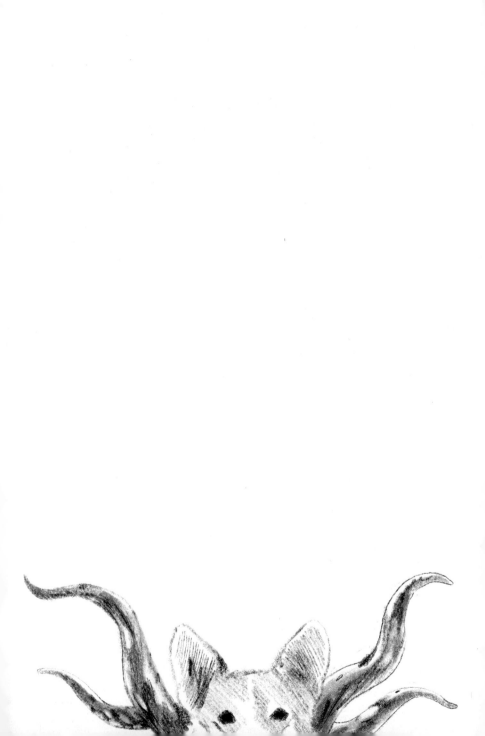

TO BE CONTINUED IN

HELL DIFFICULTY TUTORIAL

VOLUME 2